COLLISION AT ROOSEVELT RANCH

ROOSEVELT RANCH BOOK THREE

ELISE FABER

COLLISION AT ROOSEVELT RANCH
BY ELISE FABER
Newsletter sign-up
This is a work of fiction. Names, places, characters, and events are fictitious in
every regard. Any similarities to actual events and persons, living or dead, are
purely coincidental. Any trademarks, service marks, product names, or named
features are assumed to be the property of their respective owners, and are used
only for reference. There is no implied endorsement if any of these terms are
used. Except for review purposes, the reproduction of this book in whole or part,
electronically or mechanically, constitutes a copyright violation.

ROOSEVELT RANCH SERIES

Disaster at Roosevelt Ranch

Heartbreak at Roosevelt Ranch

Collision at Roosevelt Ranch

Regret at Roosevelt Ranch

Desire at Roosevelt Ranch

For "fucking bubbles"
Because sometimes you just need to burst them . . .

ONE

Haley

"Just play already," Haley muttered, fumbling with her phone as she pulled to a stop at an intersection on her way home from the hospital. It was late and she was tired and . . . she just wanted some boy band love, okay?

Exhaustion tugged at her brain and she sighed, eyes burning, shoulders aching. She was very close to tears.

She'd lost a patient that night.

It hadn't been her fault. It hadn't been *anyone's* fault. Sometimes those things just happened—accidents, everyone working frantically to pull someone back from the brink, a body failing—but that didn't make a patient dying on her watch any easier.

Her job was to save them.

Life was fragile. As a nurse, Haley knew that firsthand. But she'd also left her job at the busy county hospital in California and returned home to Darlington, Utah because she was tired of seeing people die every day.

She was damned good at compartmentalizing, but some things weren't so easy to shove down.

Sometimes those fuckers—e.g. *memories*—kept popping back up.

And sometimes the cases hit too close to home—

A horn beeped behind her and she jumped. "Shit." Her phone was still not cooperating, the poppy upbeat notes of her favorite boy bands remaining silently trapped inside the technological device that never seemed to work correctly.

Even though it was brand spanking new.

Even though she'd gotten a complete tutorial from her brother-in-law, who had gone through all of the troubleshooting with her.

Even though the freaking tech from the phone store had personally tested the Bluetooth by coming out to her car and showing her how it worked.

Technology. She repelled it.

Or rather, she was technology's kryptonite.

Two minutes around her, and she destroyed even the most powerful device.

"Yay me," she murmured, dropping the phone to her passenger's seat. Haley shouldn't be fussing with it anyway, not while she was driving, but—*sigh*—she'd really wanted to escape for the rest of her drive.

Apparently, that was not to be.

Checking for traffic, she pulled carefully through the intersection. Darlington was a small town, and signals were few and far between, but the roads at this time of the night were dark . . . and she'd had a deer jump right in front of her car once before.

The car that had honked at her turned to follow her down the bumpy lane, headlights very bright in her rearview mirror, the front bumper just inside that bubble all drivers had.

This one triggered her slightly-too-close alert but not the this-fucker-better-back-off alarm.

Her lips curved.

So, she might have gotten used to the more aggressive drivers of Northern California.

The thought of her first months in San Francisco, of the busy roads, the huge buildings, the patient care that both challenged and devastated her, brought a smile to her face. For all the reasons she'd come home, Haley was still happy she'd left Utah for a time.

Small town life was . . . well, small.

Or it had seemed that way before she'd left.

Now she saw how much her world had expanded by being . . . well, herself. Having *found* herself, as cliché as that sounded.

She'd left a little girl, never feeling like she could measure up, and had returned—

Still feeling like she would never live up to her expectations.

Ha. Well, that was life for a girl. But Haley *had* come back with the understanding that she was the one setting impossible standards. Progress, yes? As in, *she* was a work in progress.

Step one was realizing that not everything she did had to be perfect and exacting.

Which was all well and good for her Pinterest attempts —*cough*—fails.

It didn't work as well for her patients.

Hence the mental punch fest happening in her brain alongside the compelling need for cheesy pop music to provide her with some escapism.

Had she done everything right? What had she missed? What could she have done differently? Would any of it have made any difference?

No.

No, it wouldn't have.

Tears stung her eyes, and she blinked them away.

If Haley hadn't blinked at that moment, things might not have turned out as they did.

But she *did* blink, right as two other things happened simultaneously.

Music exploded through her speakers—the Backstreet Boys singing about the way they wanted it—and a deer jumped into the road.

By the time her lids had flashed back open, the jar of pop-tastic noise accelerating the process to near inhuman speed, the freaking deer was directly in front of her bumper and *definitely* within her bubble.

Frankly, it was firmly in the she-was-gonna-plow-it-down-and-make-a-deer-pancake zone.

"Fuck!" She slammed on her brakes.

Tires screeched. She braced for impact and then . . .

The deer executed a leap that was fitting of a figure skater and jumped clear of her car.

Haley sighed in relief. For a single heartbeat.

Because that relief disappeared before the next.

Her body was propelled forward as the driver who had been —and here came that damned bubble analogy again—following her too closely before, plowed into her from behind.

And she didn't even have time to snort about the dirtiness of that particular innuendo before the seat belt yanked tightly across her chest. Pain shot up her leg as her foot compressed more firmly on the brake pedal, but before she could focus too much on the sensation, her head smacked against the top of the steering wheel a moment before the airbag deployed and punched her in the face.

"Fucking bubbles," she slurred as everything went black.

TWO

Sam

Sᴀᴍ ᴡᴀꜱ ᴇxʜᴀᴜꜱᴛᴇᴅ.

He'd been in surgery for hours, trying to extract every last piece of shredded plastic from the belly of a six-month-old Yellow Lab named Dexter, and it hadn't been an easy procedure. The pup was severely dehydrated and had probably been at most a day from dying.

Dexter was lucky Sam had the ability to perform an emergency surgery in his clinic and hadn't needed to be driven all the way to Salt Lake City, an almost three-hour jaunt.

It had likely saved the dog's life that evening.

But it was also why Sam was bone-weary and driving along the dark road late at night.

He'd gotten through the surgery then helped his overnight staff make sure Dexter was stable, which meant he was hours past his normal shift length.

And considering he'd gone out to Roosevelt Ranch early

that morning to check on a pregnant mare, Sam was lucky to still be coherent.

He was also in a hurry to get home and crawl into bed.

"Come on," he muttered, beeping his horn at the car in front of him. It wasn't familiar, a sleek black sedan with California plates he didn't recognize, and considering Darlington was a small town, that in itself was unusual.

Though being unfamiliar was also probably why the other driver was glancing at their phone. It was easy to get turned around out in the sticks. One wrong turn on a pitch-black lane and a car could enter a veritable Bermuda Triangle of farms, twisting roads, and hidden driveways.

Part of him felt he should offer help, but the rest was relieved when the other driver put down their phone and headed decisively to the right.

Of course, that was the direction he was going as well, though he wasn't going to complain, not when they were moving along at a good clip and his house was less than a mile ahead.

Sam could summon up some patience, at least for another few minutes.

Unfortunately for him, his phone buzzed, and as quickly as it took for his eyes to flick down to check the Caller ID then flick back up to the road, everything went to hell.

Brake lights flared bright red in front of him, casting the dark street in ghoulish repose, and the careful distance he'd been keeping between his car and the one in front of him simply . . . evaporated.

In one instant, he was way too close.

Cursing, he slammed on the brakes and swerved to the right.

He almost missed the little sedan.

What was the saying? *Almost* only counts in horseshoes and hand grenades?

Yeah. That was it. And the noise his SUV made crashing into the car in front of him was what he imagined a grenade going off sounded like.

The crunching of fiberglass meeting his metal bumper.

Glass shattering. Metal screeching.

Add in the squealing of his tires and the hissing of his engine after he'd come to a full stop, and he half expected to look out his cracked windshield and find that a war zone had materialized in the few heartbeats that had passed during the collision.

No war zone.

But there wasn't any sign of movement from the other car.

"Fuck," he muttered and shoved open his door. It took a hell of a lot of effort, which probably meant that with his luck, the frame was bent and his SUV would be totaled.

But none of that mattered.

He ran over to the sedan and glanced through the window.

The airbag had deployed, and the driver was slumped against the steering wheel and the rapidly deflating white nylon.

A long blond ponytail trailed down the woman's back, bisecting a medical scrub top that was patterned with galosh-wearing pigs.

His heart dropped, and he yanked open the door.

Because . . . Haley.

Horrible music blared through the speakers, and he winced as he checked Haley's pulse. It was strong, if a little elevated. Of course, then there was the fact that she was unconscious.

"Damn," he muttered, seeing the blood on the steering wheel. Guilt had already been flowing pretty free and loose through him, but now Sam felt even worse.

He'd hurt Haley.

"Fuck."

He whipped out his phone and called the emergency line at the police department, otherwise known as Rob Cooper, lead detective at the Darlington Sheriff's office.

"Rob speaking," he answered, voice clear despite the late hour.

"It's Sam. There's—"

"You up past bedtime karaoke-ing boy bands again?"

Sam snorted. "Hilarious. Now shut it. There's been an accident on Old Creek Rd. I rear-ended Haley Donovan, and she's unconscious." He sucked in a breath, checked for the mile marker and relayed that as well. "Can you send an ambulance?"

To Rob's credit, the man could switch gears with the best of them. He was also calm in a crisis. Then again, he'd had plenty of experience in dealing with them. Plus, Sam knew he'd be able to get an ambulance out faster than just him calling 9-1-1 on his own. Rob was unruffled, had good connections, and could directly coordinate with dispatch.

Haley groaned and started to push up.

"I'm getting off the line now," he told Rob. "She's coming around."

"Ambulance is on its way," Rob said then, "Don't move her unless you have to."

"Roger that." Sam hung up and pocketed his cell just as Haley flopped back in her seat. "Careful," he told her. "You—"

Fuck.

He'd seen the blood but not the large gash marring her forehead. Not to mention the fact that her face was going to bruise to hell and back over the next few days.

"Hold still," he ordered, shrugging out of his shirt and folding it quickly to make a compress. "You're bleeding."

"What's the matter?" Her hands came up to bat his away when he pressed it to the cut above her eye. "*Stop.* That hurts."

"Haley. Hold. Still," he ordered again and kept the pad firmly in place. Of course, the damned woman did not *hold still*, but at least she stopped trying to knock his hands off. "You were in an accident—"

She shook her head, as though trying to clear it. "Sam?" Her eyes finally focused on his. "I was in an accident? What happened? Did I lose consciousness?"

"Yes. I rear-ended your car when you slammed on the brakes. And yes," he gritted, "you were out for a couple of minutes. Now stop fighting me and hold this"—he brought her hands up to the compress—"so I can shut off the damned music."

"I'm not fighting you," she said, but because she finally did freeze, Sam didn't bother arguing further with her. Instead, he just reached over her and pressed the power button on her stereo.

The music kept playing.

"It never cooperates," she muttered. "Scared the crap out of me—"

"That's why you slammed on the brakes?" Sam asked, pressing the nob again.

The music played on. Another band crooning about how it better be them.

"Well, that, plus the fucking deer teleporting in front of my car," she grumbled. "How long was I out?"

He tried turning down the volume knob. Nothing. "A couple of minutes at most."

"My head wound?"

"You'll need stitches and a CT." She started shaking her head, and Sam leaned back, glaring at her. "You nauseous?"

Her lips pressed flat.

"Head wound. Loss of consciousness. Nausea? Dizziness? A killer headache?" Those lips stayed firmly flattened. "I'm guessing I'm right, and so as a nurse, if you had a patient with these symptoms, what would you tell them?"

Silence.

"Exactly."

She huffed. "My phone is on the floor." She pointed to the passenger's side. "You might be able to turn it off that way."

"Stay." Another order as he made his way around the car and opened the passenger door. Sure enough, her cell was on the floor and was miraculously undamaged. He pressed the button on its side, swiped up and turned off the Bluetooth.

Blessed silence rang out around them.

Which was promptly punctuated by sirens.

Haley sighed and glared over at him. "I'm guessing that's my ride?"

THREE

Haley

So as far as embarrassments went, being wheeled into the hospital on a gurney, when she could damn well walk—okay, so maybe it was more like limp. Anyway, walking ability or not, being brought into her place of work on a squeaking stretcher, was pretty much right up there with her most cringe-worthy moments.

Especially since the small town Emergency Department was quiet and everyone blatantly watched as she was pushed in.

Roxy, the nurse who'd relieved her barely an hour before, grinned as she was pushed by. "Couldn't stay away?"

Dr. Hamilton was in charge that evening. He clapped his hands together, pretending to send a prayer up to the heavens. "Finally, something to do."

What was that about ER staff and dark senses of humor?

Oh yeah.

They all had it.

And in that exact moment their peculiar sense of comedy was *hil-ar-i-ous*.

Yes, she got it. She knew that while the hospital just outside Darlington had its rare moments of busy—though that was certainly still relative when compared to the county hospital in San Francisco that she'd left—it was more often quiet than slammed. She also knew that it had been exceptionally quiet that evening by the time she'd left.

So much so that had Haley been working, she would have looked at any arriving patient with the same amount of benefaction.

"Not much to do," she told them. "Stitches and maybe a sprained ankle."

Both of which meant that she probably wouldn't be able to work the next day.

Dammit.

That meant she'd be required to put in an appearance at Sunday dinner.

Fuck. Her. Life.

"It's something," Dr. Hamilton—*Julian*—said. "I need to practice my sutures."

Haley shuddered at the thought of being his guinea pig. "Dude. You're supposed to perfect them in medical school."

Lips twitched. "Maybe I'm out of practice."

Considering that although Julian was young and fresh out of his residency, he was one of the smartest and well-rounded doctors she'd ever met, Haley had no doubt his stitches would be more precise than a fashion designer's.

"Not likely," she said, pushing up to sit as the gurney was situated next to a bed and sliding herself over before the paramedics, Dean and Kristin, could help her. She was a nurse, dammit. She could move two feet, but even Haley had to admit that those two feet were really fucking painful. "Thanks, guys," she told the paramedics, waving as they left and hiding her wince, pretending her ankle wasn't a throbbing mess that was making her head spin.

Or maybe that was the head wound.

"Ten bucks there's a fracture in that ankle."

Sam's voice made her gaze fly to the open door. She hadn't expected him to come to the hospital. He'd been dealing with the police as she'd been packed into the back of the ambulance, all while declaring that she didn't need the transport, that she wasn't that bad off and could drive herself into the hospital.

Kristin hadn't even argued with her. She'd just nodded at Dean and the two of them had bundled her onto the gurney and off to the ER on the red-and-white express.

Thankfully they hadn't used the siren.

Small victories. Haley was all about them.

"It's just a sprain," she said with a glare, already thinking about how big the hospital bills were going to be. First, Sam crashed into her car, *then* he called 9-1-1—

Okay, so maybe if she hadn't slammed on the brakes . . .

Details. Details.

One of Sam's dark brown brows rose as if to say, "We'll see."

Yeah, they *would* see, wouldn't they?

Meanwhile, Julian and Roxy bustled around her—Julian putting in orders for X-rays and medications, while Roxy started a line and then hung a bag of antibiotics and fluid . . . and a little something for pain relief.

Sam stood unobtrusively in the corner.

Though he'd never been unobtrusive to her.

Haley's childhood crush hadn't changed. In fact, he was prettier than ever, more muscular and filled out and just . . . completely yummy and male.

He'd owned her heart the first time he'd helped her with her history homework, way back when she'd been in seventh grade and he'd been in eleventh. Sam had been gorgeous then, all long, lean lines and possessing a smile that made her stomach fill with butterflies.

Of course, he'd also been dating her sister Maggie, so that had been a problem.

Especially since he'd practically lived at her house for years because they'd dated all the way through high school and college. His constancy in her life meant that her crush had *years* to develop into something so painful and awkward and soul-crushing that she'd been determined to leave town when he and Maggie got married.

Only he and Maggie *hadn't* gotten married.

He'd left for vet school, and her sister had stayed.

No wedding. No more Sam.

Except, he'd returned to Darlington . . . and now so had she.

"Fuck," she murmured and forced her mind from the past.

"Sorry," Julian said gentling his touch on her forehead.

She didn't have the strength to tell him that his touch wasn't what was hurting her. Hell, by now she was floating on some good drugs and hadn't even felt Roxy cleaning the wound.

Her ankle still throbbed though.

Ugh.

Because that probably meant Sam was right.

Instead of going further down that particular train of thought, Haley shut her mouth and held very still as Julian closed up her forehead.

As predicted his stitches were perfectly straight.

"I told you," she said as she snuck a quick glance with her phone. Sam had returned it after managing to make turning off her playlist look as simple as pressing a button.

Technology. It hated her.

"Told me what?" Julian asked.

"That your sutures are perfect." She grinned at him. "In fact, they're fashion-designer worthy."

"I hear the mummy look is in right now," Roxy chimed in, holding up a roll of gauze before bandaging Haley's wound.

Haley rolled her eyes, and the motion meant she caught another glimpse of Sam in the corner.

Dammit, why was the man so fucking hot?

Even in the fluorescent lighting, his skin was a gorgeous tawny brown and his eyes resembled melted dark chocolate, while she knew hers bore a strong resemblance to mud.

Gross, sticky mud filled with horse manure.

Okay, so she was being dramatic.

But, really, the man was supermodel beautiful and despite having broken her sister's heart once upon a time, he'd grown into a seriously nice guy. The type to stop and pull over if he saw an old lady struggling to load her groceries in her car or to shovel his neighbor's driveway just because he happened to be outside digging out his own.

He was sweet. Kind. Sexy and—

It didn't matter.

Even if he did see her as a woman and not the awkward, gangly sister of an old flame, he was in the no-touch zone.

Fuck. Between bubbles and zones, she was losing her mind.

But there was a sister code and that meant no dating exes. Not ever. Even if it had been close to a decade since their broken engagement. Even though her sister was happily married to someone else.

Nope. No way.

She couldn't muddy the waters.

Not that Sam wanted to muddy them with her.

"Men," she muttered and Roxy, who'd been clearing off the rolling table, snorted before patting her shoulder. "I feel ya, girl." Her eyes flicked to Sam then back to Haley. "I'll come back when X-Ray is ready for you."

Haley nodded then gave Julian a thumbs up when he told her he'd check on her after the results were in and hurried from the room.

He'd just been notified that another patient was en route.

Which meant that the occupancy of the ER was about to double.

Sam pushed off the wall and moved toward her, drawing her gaze as easily as a bar of Godiva at a Chocolaholics Anonymous meeting.

Oh, look there she went again being ridiculous.

But shoving her mind down a track that had nothing to do with Sam and everything to do with ridiculous analogies had been her survival technique for years.

Yes, she could compartmentalize. No problem. Sam Johnson wasn't even in the room as far as she was concerned. It was all milk versus dark chocolate and—

Dammit, now Sam's *dark chocolate* eyes were on hers, his slightly roughened fingertips brushing across the back of her hand.

"I'm sorry you got hurt because of me."

The sheer amount of remorse in his voice pulled her out of her whirling mind. He felt bad? *She'd* slammed on the brakes.

"You do realize that it's the deer we both should be pissed at, right?"

His brows drew down. "I should have been paying closer attention." With a sigh, he straightened and turned, pacing away. "I should have given you more space, and I should have made sure I was more alert—"

"When the Backstreet Boys blared to roaring life on my speakers at the same time that a deer decided to try and commit death by front bumper?" She fixed him with a glare. "You should have known at that exact moment to slow down *and* be more awake?" Shoving her elbows under herself, she went to sit up, only to make it halfway before collapsing back down with a moan.

Sam whipped around. "Are you all right?"

"Fine," she said, keeping her eyes closed and waiting for the room to stop spinning.

He touched her shoulder "I think you probably have a concussion."

"So does Julian," she said, eyes still closed. "He wrote it in my chart."

"Hmm," Sam said.

Her lids pulled back. "What?"

"*Julian?*" he asked, so smirky and all-knowing.

She rolled her eyes. "He's too young for me."

Sam huffed. "Haley, you're all of—"

"Twenty-seven."

His jaw dropped open. "No, you're not."

Really? She narrowed her eyes, talking slowly to break it down for the infuriating man. "You, thirty-two. Me, twenty-seven. That's how math works."

"How did that—" He broke off.

"Happen?" she said. "Life, Sam. Life."

"Damn." He blew out a breath. "Still, life or not, I really *am* sorry I crashed into you.

Haley rolled her eyes. "Can we agree to just blame the deer?" Silence met her question, and she stifled a sigh. "And I didn't mean that Julian is too young age-wise for me. I just meant that he's too young . . . I don't know, soul-wise? Personality-wise? Does that even make sense?"

"No."

She opened her mouth to snap at him then saw the corners of his lips twitching. "God, you're just the same."

"No," he said, and his tone took on a hint of darkness that had her frowning as she tried to interpret it. Of course, that frown was followed quickly by a wince as her stitches pulled, distracting her from the topic at hand. And she was further veered from the blip of pain from Sam's past when he said, "But I do understand not shitting where you eat."

"Barf," she quipped before shrugging. "Not the most pleasant saying, but it is apt, especially in this case. I don't date people from the hospital. It's too complicated." Not to mention the dating pool was pretty small and also that she had sworn off men at the moment. After Brian—

Yeah.

Nope.

Not going there.

"I think Julian is technically a few years older than me in years," she said. "But much younger in life experience. At least outside of a hospital setting. Does that make more sense?"

Sam stared at her. And cue more silence, this time of the growing-more-awkward-by-the-second variety.

So, when exactly would it be rude for her to ask him to leave?

It wasn't that she wanted to be alone necessarily, but between the past and the awkward present and then adding in the dark circles beneath his eyes, it was probably better if they just parted ways and returned to being casual acquaintances.

Sam was as tired as she was. He needed rest. Not to pass a couple of uncomfortable hours in a hospital with a girl he knew from the past.

He might be a good guy, but he wasn't hers.

And it was critical that she remembered that.

"You should go," she murmured.

"I'm not—"

Roxy bustled back in at that moment, cutting off what

would no doubt be a protest. Sam was a good guy and wouldn't dare to leave a damsel in distress. "X-Ray is ready for you."

"Great," she said as Roxy unlocked the gurney. "You really should go," she added as her friend started to wheel her out.

His eyes flashed. "You need—"

"Go, Sam." She made a shooing motion. "I'm fine here." When he looked like he would argue further, Haley fixed him with a glare. "Seriously. I'm. Fine."

"It'll be a little while before the on-call ortho can read the X-Rays anyway," Roxy added, and Haley could have kissed her.

"Fine." Sam threw up his hands. "I'll go. Call me if you need—"

"I'll be fine," she said.

He shook his head, following the gurney out. But where Roxy and Haley turned right to head to X-Ray, Sam turned left and headed for the exit.

The blip of regret she felt, the little aching slice as he disappeared from sight, was familiar.

She was used to Sam Johnson walking away from her.

Though, this time Haley knew it was because she'd pushed him.

It was better for everyone that way.

FOUR

Sam

HE WALKED AROUND THE CORNER, paused and waited for the nurse to wheel Haley through the opposite doors.

Then he rotated around and strode back toward her room.

The doctor—*Julian*, he thought with a huff—came out of another patient's room. "Everything all right?"

Sam gave the other man a commiserating look. "Haley doesn't want to inconvenience me by having me stay." Okay, only a half-truth. She'd ordered him to leave, but he wasn't about to abandon her while she was concussed and sporting stitches, as well as a broken ankle.

And he'd seen enough broken bones to know that ankle was definitely fractured.

Julian nodded. "She's stubborn, that one. A hell of a nurse, though."

Sam didn't doubt that. Even as kids she'd been smart as hell, strong, quick-thinking, and possessed a streak of empathy that fit very well with her current occupation.

"But," Julian went on, "at the same time, she doesn't want you here—"

"I'll stay out of the way and keep quiet," Sam said. He appreciated that the doctor was willing to go to bat for Haley, but—"I just want to make sure she gets home safely."

Julian studied him for a beat. "I'm leaving it up to her," he said after a long moment. "If she wants you gone, I'll make sure you're gone."

There was steel in the other man's tone that Sam respected. Though it seemed at odds with the youthful naiveté Haley had described. Maybe there was more to Julian than she'd grasped.

Not that Sam would be railroaded into leaving. It was his fault that Haley was hurt, so he'd make certain she was safe and secure at home and then he'd crash—

Er, get some shut-eye.

But instead of saying any of that, he nodded—Julian could interpret that however he wanted—and continued back down the hall to Haley's room. Once inside, he plunked down into a chair and pulled out his phone.

Typically, he kept to a light schedule on Sundays. Some office visits for the clients who couldn't make it in during normal hours, a few home visits for horses or cattle on the surrounding ranches. But he saw with no little amount of relief that his schedule was completely clear.

Probably because Jane had known how late he'd worked that evening.

Sam glanced at the clock on his phone's screen and saw that it was nearly the *previous* evening at that point.

He knew Haley worked days and wondered why she'd been leaving work so late, especially based on the quiet Emergency Department surrounding him.

Maybe it had been busy earlier.

So, aside from checking in on Dexter, making sure the pup

was still looking good after surgery, all he needed to do the next day was make sure that Haley was okay.

He could do that.

As long as he didn't hit her with his car again.

Snorting, he passed the time waiting for Haley by checking some sports scores on his cell. He'd gone to veterinary school in Minnesota and had become a bit of a hockey fan, though his fandom didn't actually extend to the state's teams.

His love of hockey had begun during the league's most recent expansion and as thus, he'd been following the San Francisco Gold since their very first season.

They'd begun shakily but were damned good now.

Of course, they were also currently helmed by the league's only engaged couple, Brit Plantain and Stefan Barie.

Sam was a sucker for their story—the first female player in the NHL and the captain of the team they both played for falling in love.

So, he was a romantic.

Haters were gonna hate.

Rolling his eyes at himself, Sam saw the Gold had won that evening and noted their position in the West. Playoff hopes were high, though it was still too early in the season for them to know for sure.

He hoped they did well, because he really wanted Brit to win a Cup.

Feminist *and* romantic. See? He was owning his Millennial status.

Throw in some avocado toast, and he was there.

He'd just pocketed his phone when he heard Haley's voice echo down the hall. Bracing himself for her reaction, Sam stood.

The same nurse wheeled the gurney in, and he knew the exact moment Haley saw him. Her words cut off, her eyes flashed, and red painted itself across her cheekbones.

"I thought I told you to leave."

The nurse sucked in a breath. "Harsh, girl."

"Shut it, Roxy," Haley snapped, though it held little heat, and the words were slightly slurred. "This one is trouble."

Sam helped Roxy position the bed and lock the wheels in place. "I did leave," Sam said. "I just came back."

Roxy—a women with shining black hair, curves for days, and a smile that seemed to light up the room—smirked at Haley. "You've got a live one with this one."

"Tell me about it," Haley muttered. "He was hot as hell then and even better looking full-grown."

Roxy's brows raised. "Full-grown?"

"Big. Bigger." She lifted a hand loosely gesturing some-where in the direction of Sam's crotch.

Though he was inclined to believe she was referring to his height.

"*And* he broke my sister's heart."

Fuck. He and Maggie had been over for a decade. They'd—

"Holy drugs, Batman," Roxy said.

"Told you I was a lightweight." Her eyes slid closed.

"That you did." Roxy fiddled with the computer for a moment. "I'll drop your dosage." When Haley's eyes stayed shut and her breathing evened out, the nurse turned to face Sam. "Her ankle's broken."

Nailed it, he thought like an eight-year-old, but instead of saying that aloud he just nodded.

"It's not bad," Roxy added. "The tech will be in soon to cast it. Then you can get her home since she's clearly in no shape to drive."

"Works for me." He'd managed to drive his car to the hospi-tal, but he'd definitely need to get a mechanic to look at the door . . . not to mention to find out if the unpleasant grinding sound it had made when in motion was indeed a bent frame or something less serious.

Roxy pressed a few more buttons on the keyboard then started to walk from the room. At the threshold of the doorway, she paused and glanced back at him. "Did you really break her sister's heart?"

Sam clenched his teeth tightly together. "I think it was more of a mutual shattering."

She studied him for a long moment but only said, "Hmm."

Then Roxy walked out, leaving him alone with a drugged-out Haley and just one thought running on repeat through his brain.

Haley thought he'd gotten even better looking.

Hmm, was right.

FIVE

Haley

"I DON'T NEED—"

Her protest was cut off as Roxy shut the door of Sam's SUV right in her face.

"Help," she finished, rather unnecessarily since she was talking to herself in the empty car.

Sam rounded the hood, heading for the driver's side, and she sighed for what felt like the hundredth time that day. The truth was Haley was exhausted and wanted nothing more than to collapse into bed, fall headlong into sleep, and pretend this day hadn't happened.

The driver's door stuck for a few seconds, Sam playing tug-of-war with it until it popped open, the overhead lights of the cab seeming to spotlight the cast on her right leg.

Yup. Broken.

Just as Sam had said.

Wonderful.

How the hell was she going to get to work? Hell, how in the *hell* was she going to leave her house to get groceries or toilet paper? She lived miles from the center of town and—

She was going to have to call her *mother*.

Why did Fate hate her so much?

"You okay?" Sam asked softly as he turned on the car and carefully backed out of the stall.

"Great," she said cheerily.

Just freaking out about being isolated and her cupboards being bare, since she'd planned to go shopping tomorrow . . . or rather later today.

Just cringing at the dressing down her mom was going to give her upon finding out that she'd been in an accident and hadn't—gasp of all the *freaking* gasps—called her.

Just feeling rubbed raw inside, not only from her injuries but because she'd lost a patient only hours before and then been in an accident.

The SUV came to a stop, and fingers brushed over her forehead. "Your leg is hurting you."

No.

Yes.

"It's fine," she eventually answered.

Haley was a bundle of tangled emotions and sensations—part adrenaline letdown, part throbbing pain from her ankle and head, part discomfort from the past rearing its fucking head, and all . . . regret.

She'd lost someone under her care, that was the worst of it.

But also weighing on her was the fact that it had been a decade, and she was right back where she'd started. Still mooning after her sister's ex, her body irrevocably drawn to his, her heart softening despite everything that had happened with the previous men in her life.

"It's a quick drive," he said and turned his eyes back to the road.

Not one flicker of mutual attraction, not one word about her drug-induced declaration of his sexiness.

Sam was gorgeous as ever, and he still thought of her as an asexual little tagalong.

One that slammed on the brakes to avoid a deer.

One that couldn't work technology and succumbed to the blaring soundwaves of the Backstreet Boys by braking even harder.

Le. Sigh.

They turned right onto Old Creek Road.

Sam flicked his gaze toward hers. "You're at the Robertson's—"

Her eyes caught a flicker of—

"Watch out!" she shrieked, pointing through the windshield.

He slammed on the brakes, and the SUV came to a shuddering stop inches from a deer.

That had jumped into the middle of the road.

Again.

Did all the ungulates in this area have a fucking death wish?

She and Sam looked at each other.

"Can we blame the deer now?"

His lips twitched. "Yes, I guess we can."

The buck loped away, disappearing into the brush along the side of the road. After a moment, Sam cautiously accelerated and continued with his question, though this time he kept his eyes firmly on the road. "You're at the Robertson's old place, right?"

She nodded, heart still pounding, and because she didn't want to risk another Deer-gate, she also said aloud, "Yup. The second driveway past yours."

"Got it." A beat of quiet then, "Backstreet Boys are still your favorite band?"

Her groan made him chuckle. "No, for the record, my musical taste has miraculously expanded beyond boy bands," she said. "I even like a few female pop stars now."

Now it was his turn to groan. "What about the classics?"

"You mean those eighties hair bands you used to be obsessed with?" she teased, falling into their old, yet very familiar pattern —arguing about her horrible taste in music as compared to his completely different, albeit still horrible, preference. "Give me a fun, upbeat song on the radio any day of the week. It doesn't have to be deep or soul-wrenching. I just need a slice of escapism."

He drove past his driveway, slowing down as he neared the one that led to her little ranch. She only had a couple of acres, the Robertson's having sold off most of their acreage to a neighbor when they had retired, but the tiny bunkhouse had been the perfect size for her.

Weekend DIY projects for the win.

"And why did you need the escapism today?" he asked.

Her heart squeezed. "I didn't say I needed—"

"You were listening to "I Want it That Way" at full volume. Fifteen years ago, that meant your boyfriend had dumped you." He flicked on the signal and cautiously executed the turn onto her driveway, as though half expecting another deer to jump out at any point during the maneuver.

Frankly, after their last two experiences, that wasn't a criticism.

Her own eyes were darting around, ready to reveal any deer kamikazes.

"I wasn't dumped."

"So, you and Brian are still together?"

Her jaw dropped open. "How do you know about Brian?"

"Maggie and I catch up every now and then." A shrug. "Apparently, your parents really like him."

"Yeah, well, they *really* like any man who might potentially marry me and knock me up." She sighed, reaching to unlatch her seat belt when Sam pulled to a stop in front of her house. "And not even in that order, as my mom stressed to me the last time I went over for dinner." Haley affected her mother's slightly shrill and very demanding tone. "I need more grandbabies, and it's your turn to have them. I don't even care if you have them without a husband."

Thanks, Mom.

Sam winced.

"Exactly," she muttered, popping her door.

"Hang on." He hurried out of his side then reached into the back for her crutches. Moving around the front of the car, he opened her door and helped her out, steadying her as she got her crutches under her.

He also had a knee scooter in his trunk, but considering her driveway was gravel, it wouldn't be much help except inside her house.

The crutches dug into her armpits, but she ignored the pain and took one faltering step in the direction of her front door. Between the uneven surface of the gravel and the leftover light-headedness from the quote-unquote *good drugs* Roxy had given her, the wobble factor was legit.

"Don't hate me," Sam said, after she'd managed one more shaky movement. He swept her up into his arms, letting the crutches fall to the ground. "I'll come back for them."

Less than ten seconds later, she was at her front door and Sam was retrieving her keys from her purse, then she was inside her house and directing him toward her bedroom.

Directing Sam Johnson to *her* bedroom.

Yeah, get a laugh out of that one, universe.

Gently, he set her on her mattress then straightened. "Want me to grab you some pajamas?"

"God, yes," she said and pointed to her dresser. "Top drawer."

She blamed the drugs for not remembering that was also her underwear drawer. As in, it was filled with loads of very skimpy thongs and lacy bras she'd bought in anticipation of the wedding night and honeymoon she'd been going to have with Brian.

Sam pulled open the drawer and froze.

Haley knew her cheeks were fire-engine red. "Just the shorts and tank top on the right."

He coughed. "Right," he repeated, and a moment later he slid the dresser closed with a *thunk* before turning to face her. "Uh . . . should I call Brian?"

Fuck. How many more times was he going to mention Brian?

"Brian and I aren't together, okay?" she snapped. "He fucked around with one of my good friends, and I broke things off."

Sam's eyes narrowed. "He did what?"

She made a disgusted noise. "It doesn't matter. The only thing that does is that he's not in my life, and I'm sure as shit not going to call him."

"Your mom?"

The look she shot Sam should have eviscerated him.

"Okay, so not your mom." He crossed over to her. "Do you want me to call Maggie?"

"Sam," she said. "It's nearly one in the morning, and my sister has three young kids. I'm not waking her up for a few stitches and a barely broken bone."

"You shattered your ankle."

She huffed. "Two bones. And they're hardly shattered," she grumbled. "The orthopedist didn't even recommend surgery."

"You *want* surgery?"

Her eyes rolled heavenward. "Of course not! My point is, I'm fine. It's not serious. Telling them can wait until everyone has had a full night's sleep."

"You were transported by ambulance."

"And whose fault is that?" she said, gesturing him to turn around. He did so, though not quickly enough for her to miss the remorseful expression on his face and then feel guilty in exchange. "I didn't mean *that*," she said, carefully working her scrub top up and over the bandage on her head. "The accident was just that: an accident. I was referring to the ambulance ride and how unnecessary it was."

"You were unconscious."

Her day got loads better because she unhooked her bra and tossed it to the side before slipping on her tank top. "Yeah. I get *why* you called." A sigh. "I'm just not looking forward to paying the bill."

He started to face her again.

"Stop," she ordered, having already worked her pants down over the cast. "I'm half-naked over here."

Sam froze, face still pointed toward the wall. "Do you need money?" he asked after a moment."

"No," Haley answered truthfully. "It's not the money." She slipped off her underwear then tugged on the shorts. "It's just . . . embarrassing, I guess, my coworkers seeing me like that."

He considered her words for a long moment then said, "You still think you need to be invincible, don't you?"

Fuck.

How did he always know?

How was he *always* able to see straight into the heart of her and understand?

"I'm decent," she said, instead of answering him. "I'll call

Maggie in the morning. Would you mind leaving the crutches at the foot of the bed along with the scooter?"

He rotated around. "I'll sleep on the couch," he said, moving over to help her adjust her blankets over her. "Just in case you need anything."

Now that sounded like an extra circle of hell, specially designed for her.

"No, Sam." She firmed her voice. "You've done enough already. Just leave the crutches and scooter then go home and crash. I'll be fine."

He raised a brow as he bent over and leveled serious eyes on her. "So, what you're saying is that you want me to go home and worry about you being here all alone? Worry so much that I'll toss and turn and—"

"You're laying it on thick." Exhaustion was creeping at the edges of her vision, and the one thing she *really* wanted to do at that moment was sleep, not argue with Sam.

He held up his phone.

"Either I stay on the couch or I call Maggie and wake her up."

Eyes drooping, Haley rolled her head to the side on the pillow and glared up at him. "Blackmail is how we're playing this thing?"

"Less blackmail and more making you see sense."

"Po-tay-to. Po-tah-to," she muttered. "Fine. You're on the couch, but only for tonight and because if you risked driving down to your house again, you'd have to navigate the deer gauntlet." Her lids blinked closed, and she had to force herself to focus. "Extra pillows and"—a wide yawn—"blankets are in my closet."

"Sleep now, Haley Bear," he said, brushing a kiss to her cheek. "I'll find them."

A decade ago, the kiss would have filled her with equal parts joy and liquid hot embarrassment. Such a painful crush she'd had.

But tonight, she was too tired to do anything aside from snuggling into her pillow and murmuring, "That nickname is seriously the worst."

Sam's chuckles chased her mind as sleep sucked her under.

SIX

Sam

SAM WOKE with an aching back and cramped legs.

Groaning, he stretched and rolled over then shot to rapid alertness as he nearly toppled off Haley's couch. He'd forgotten where he was.

And that was on Haley's ridiculously small love seat.

He pushed up to sitting and extended his arms over his head, tilting his head from side to side to work out the kinks.

Damn, he was getting too old to sleep in places that were not his bed.

Light streamed in through the windows, indicating it was well past his normal wake-up time of dawn. He stared out the clear pane of glass, enjoying the unobstructed view of undulating hills all colored dark green. The snow had melted, and spring was just around the corner.

Soon, he'd be spending almost as much time on the ranches helping with cattle as he did at the vet's office.

Luckily, he'd managed to hire another vet. Although Michelle would only be working part-time after coming back from maternity leave, Sam felt lucky to have wooed her over from the clinic in Campbell, a neighboring town.

Even though he loved seeing his human and domestic animal clients on a daily basis, his heart was truly with the larger livestock. There was something about the cattle and horses and, in rare cases, the bison, that drew him in.

Because they were generally less understood? Or just a bigger puzzle to solve? Or maybe even because their cases challenged his brain more?

Yes, to all.

But also, it got him out of the office and into the fields. He could feel the wind in his hair, the sun on his skin, and smell the various, though not always pleasant, scents.

Sam stood and picked up his phone. No missed calls overnight, that was good. He'd been so exhausted by the time he'd finally settled on the couch, that he worried he might sleep through an emergency.

Thankfully, no emergencies were to be had.

He sent a quick text to the night staff to check on Dexter then made his way into Haley's kitchen to rustle up some breakfast.

The rustling itself ran into a hiccup approximately two seconds after opening the fridge. As in, it was almost empty—a bottle of ketchup and a jar of pickles the only occupants. Swinging the door closed, Sam pulled out his phone and started making a list of the groceries Haley would need.

Milk. Bread. Cheese. Fruit. He wondered if she still liked bananas. When he'd been with Maggie, Haley had eaten them in near inhuman quantities. He drifted around the kitchen, pulling open cupboards in search of cereal or rice or some type of food that could sustain her.

Aside from a few packets of oatmeal, the space was bare.

Either she didn't cook at home, or she was in desperate need of a grocery run.

Sam sighed. That grocery run was going to be a lot harder now that he'd broken her leg.

He added a few more things to his list then turned to head down the hall. He'd peek in and see if she wanted him to grab anything else. But just as he'd walked through the doorway, his feet skidded to a stop. A bulletin board that he'd missed the first time hung near the door and conveniently at eye level was a notepad titled "Groceries."

Tearing off the top sheet, Sam grinned when he saw the first item on the list was bananas, written all in caps and underlined twice. So, she still liked them . . . and also there were so many juvenile jokes his mind wanted to make over her love of the yellow, phallic fruit.

But he was mature and shit, so he stifled his inner twelve-year-old and made his way on quiet feet to Haley's bedroom.

Sam was extra glad for his stealth when he poked his head in and saw that she was sound asleep, her eyes closed, her lips forming an O as her breaths came slow and steady.

God. She was beautiful.

All lean curves and porcelain skin, peaches teasing the creamy color. Her hair had lightened as she'd aged and was now more platinum than golden yellow, and her eyes . . . well, when they were actually open they were a shade that always reminded him of puffs of clouds trailing across the clear sky. Not just a flat shade of blue, but with little zigzags of gray and navy and . . . he'd never seen any like them.

Somehow, without him noticing, Haley had transformed into a goddess.

Who would have thought the tiny spitfire who'd trailed him and Maggie around would have grown into . . . *her*?

And maybe that wasn't fair, maybe he'd always shoved Haley into the little sister category because it was safer. They were not quite five years apart, and he couldn't think of her as gorgeous or sexy, not as a teenager. She'd still been in middle school, and he'd been readying to leave for college.

Not to mention the small fact that he'd been dating her sister.

But he and Maggie *weren't* together anymore, and further, they'd sorted out their differences. Now Haley was grown . . . and single.

And so was he.

Maybe—

Nope. Definitely not going there.

Groceries and then breakfast. *Those* were the things he should be thinking about.

He slipped from Haley's bedroom and quietly made his way to his car. His driver's side door took some serious coaxing—and cursing—to open, but he finally managed to get in and start the engine.

Along the way, he dialed Rob, the detective at the Sheriff's office with whom he'd spoken the night before. They'd had a tenuous relationship the previous year—Sam having stepped in to offer some help to Rob's wife, Melissa, when their dog had been injured and Rob had been busy on a case.

Rob hadn't liked that, and Sam had to admit he would have been pissed if another man had stepped in to take care of *his* woman.

But both Rocco and Melissa had been hurt. That in and of itself had trumped any rules of etiquette or Bro Code or whatever.

Sam had done what he'd *had* to do.

Thankfully, Rob had eventually seen reason.

He'd managed to solve the case that had been threatening

the town as well as his family, and he and Melissa had patched things up. She'd even discussed some of their marriage hurdles in her last book.

Yes, he'd read it.

Yes, that probably meant he had way too much free time on his hands.

Or that his life was pathetically empty.

Yay for pleasant Sunday morning thoughts.

"Johnson," Rob said by way of greeting after the phone had rung a few times.

"Hey," Sam replied. "Thanks for the assist last night."

Rob scoffed. "It's my job."

"Not sure that coordinating ambulance dispatch on a Saturday night really is your job," he said. "But I appreciate it anyway."

"It got me out of the hundredth round of UNO," Rob said. "I should be thanking you." A pause then, "So you've moved on from rescuing married women to rear-ending defenseless ones?"

Sam turned onto the road that led to the center of town. "First, your wife pretty much rescued herself. And second, I blame the deer."

Rob snorted.

"Seriously," he said. "It's a problem. Another one jumped out right in front of my car when I was driving Haley home last night."

"Are you sure it was a different deer?" Rob was grinning, Sam could tell. The bastard. "Or maybe that one just really likes you."

"Third," he continued with his list, despite Rob's smartassedness, "That's gross and against the law. Not to mention, deer carry all sorts of disease-transmitting pests. Also, *fourth*, it's like the fucking deer gauntlet out here."

Rob burst out laughing. "Deer gauntlet," he repeated, almost hysterical.

"Hilarious," Sam muttered, but he was smiling. "Deer-mageddon better?"

"Hmm." Rob considered that. "Maybe Deer-pocalypse."

They both cracked up.

Eventually, Rob sobered. "But if it really is becoming a problem, I'll get someone from the city to trim back the brush along the road. Last time I was out there, it was pretty overgrown."

"Thanks, man. That should help." Sam signaled and turned into the lot for the grocery store. "We might also have to bring in Fish and Game if it continues."

"I think we might have a hotshot vet who could recommend that as necessary."

Sam smirked and agreed, and they talked a few minutes more about the logistics of that. He told Rob he'd pass along the name of his contact from the wildlife department so they could start moving Deer-gate after he got back to his house.

Ah. Small town life.

Though, Sam was much happier the Sheriff's Office was dealing with deer instead of drugs this time around.

He had the feeling they were, too.

Darlington was supposed to be a safe place to raise families and somewhere kids didn't have to worry about their moms getting kidnapped.

Melissa had been put through the wringer, that was for sure.

After saying goodbye, Sam hung up, pocketed his phone, and wrestled his door open before heading into the store. This early in the morning it was almost empty, and he breezed through Haley's list quickly, adding in a few treats—banana ice cream, banana bread, banana cake—as well as a bouquet of flowers.

Yes, he was still feeling really guilty about the accident.

Yes, he might have also been wanting to prove to her that despite what had happened between her and her fiancé and between him and her sister, there were still good guys out there.

Also—newsflash—yes, he might have wanted to show her that *he* was one of those good guys.

This was going to become a problem. He could already sense that.

But ignoring the shitshow that was no doubt barreling toward him, Sam simply added a cheeky little teddy bear to the cart and went to the register to pay.

Haley deserved to feel good.

Five minutes later, he was heading to his SUV to load up his car, leaving the cashier, who had been studying him with unhidden curiosity, behind. Five more minutes, he guessed. That was how long it would take for the question of who he'd bought the flowers and bear for to circulate around town.

Gossip had begun to move at near light speed since Esther, eighty years old if she was a day, had started a Snapchat three months before and then put out the call for any and all rumors.

She particularly liked using the detective filter, one that put her in a police hat and aviator sunglasses, while she discussed the merits of a particular theory about who was dating who or which teenager had gotten caught doing something naughty.

And because the snaps expired within a day, the whole town jumped on them the moment Esther posted.

How did he know about this?

Because he followed her.

Sam, meet sad, empty life.

Rolling his eyes at himself, he loaded the groceries into his trunk and then forced open his car door. He needed to get the SUV looked at, but for the moment it was running, and so that could wait until tomorrow.

For now, he needed to ply Haley with banana treats and flowers and try to tease a smile out of her.

Unfortunately, when he pulled up to her house and saw the scene that was unfolding there, he knew that smiles were going to be a long time coming.

SEVEN

Haley

How MANY YEARS would she spend in prison if she murdered her mother?

Would a judge understand that she'd been driven to the absolute brink and give her a lighter sentence because *her mother was driving her absolutely crazy?*

She'd woken up stiff and sore but relatively rested, all things considered. Sam had left her medicine and a glass of water within easy reach, along with her little knee scooter, which had been really considerate of him.

Of course, he hadn't locked her front door when he'd left. Which, one—this was Darlington so that was normally fine, and two—she'd probably been sleeping when he'd needed to leave and he hadn't wanted to wake her, so also fine.

What was decidedly *not* fine was the fact that the unlocked door had meant that her mother had let herself in.

Loudly and with all the drama her mother was so apt at providing.

The screech had nearly toppled Haley from her scooter as she'd made her way from the bathroom, after having cobbled together a sponge bath and wrestled her way into some sweats and a fresh T-shirt.

Forget the bra. Ain't nobody got time for that shit in that moment.

"Haley," her mother shrieked. "Your face! Oh my God, you look horrible."

"Good to see you too, Mom," Haley muttered then hissed out a pained breath when her mother pulled her into a tight hug. Her neck and shoulders were tender, and having her aching head plastered against her mom's generous bosom didn't feel all that great either. "Easy," she said, extracting herself. "I'm fine. It was so late last night, I was going to call you this morning."

"Except you didn't call!" her mom wailed. "I waited and waited, and you didn't call."

"I woke up ten minutes ago," Haley told her.

The hysterics cut out. Just like that. "Oh."

Yeah. Oh.

"Go sit down, Mom." She started to wheel herself forward. "I'll tell you everything that happened."

Her mom's blond curls bounced as she whipped her head to narrow her eyes at Haley. "*Everything?*"

"Every. Unexciting. Thing."

"Fine."

She flounced down the hall and flopped down into the armchair. Which left Haley the couch. That Sam had slept on. *Oh God.* Had he cleaned up the blankets? Did it look like a man had slept on her couch? Was there about to be another shrill rejoinder to join the first?

The wheels of her scooter squeaked as she made her way

into the family room. Three. *Squeak.* Two. *Squeak.* One. *Squeak.* Blast—

Off?

Except not, because her couch looked exactly as it had when she'd left for work the previous day, down to the throw pillows in their proper position and her fuzzy sheep-covered blanket tossed over an arm.

She carefully maneuvered herself onto the couch—with no help from her mother. But wasn't that typical? Her mom swept in to look like she was saving the day, while at the same time stealing all the focus for herself.

And leaving drama and devastation in her wake.

Yeah, there was that.

Haley slipped her phone from her pocket, saw that it was barely nine. Was it too early to go back to bed?

Yes? No?

"It's rude to be on your phone in the middle of a conversation."

She opened her mouth, about to explain that she'd only been checking the time, before realizing that was a futile response. Her mom wouldn't listen. Ignoring anything that didn't fit with her particular viewpoint or argument was her mother's superpower.

So instead, Haley pocketed the phone and sat back on the couch. "How have you been?"

"Oh, terrible," her mom said, and she was off, lamenting about how difficult her life was, how challenging it was now that her father was required to travel more than ever for work, how lonely and quiet the house was.

Haley *could* have suggested that her mom travel with her dad. As empty nesters, there wasn't any reason for her mother to stay behind in Darlington, and they could easily afford it.

But her mom wasn't interested in solving her problems.

She just enjoyed complaining about them.

So, Haley shifted slightly, propping her foot up on a pillow and letting her back sink into the couch. Immediately, her nose was surrounded with spice and male and . . . *Sam.*

Her stomach clenched, memories flooding her. Of sitting next to him on a different couch while watching a superhero movie with him and Maggie. Of a quick hug when she'd failed a really important math test. Of him wrapping his arms around her and holding her tight as she'd shed tears over a jerky boy that had never been able to compete with him in the first place.

After all these years, he still wore the same aftershave or deodorant. Or maybe, he still just always smelled like Sam.

Like home—

"Are you even listening to me?"

Fuck. Haley had missed a rare moment requiring her to comment during one of her mom's diatribes.

They were like unicorns.

All sweet and rare and shit, but never missing a chance to gore a fucker.

"I'm—"

"All I do is love you!"

Haley closed her eyes and let her head flop back against the cushions.

"I spent two full days in labor, and you just—"

Where were the Backstreet Boys now? She could use them blaring to life on her phone and drowning out the verbal lambasting right at that moment.

"Hi, Mrs. Donovan."

The sound of Sam's voice made Haley's eyes flash open. He pushed through the front door, arms laden with grocery bags, and crossed to the kitchen island to set them down.

Then he turned to face her, pity in his gaze. "Hey." A pause before a soft question. "How are you feeling?"

She started to raise one brow and winced. "Fine. Though movement of any type is excluded from that sentiment."

His mouth quirked. "Good to know. I brought you—"

"Samuel Johnson," her mother interrupted. "As I live and breathe." She pushed to her feet, and all of the shrillness she'd been using with Haley disappeared. Yup, that sharp, cajoling tone was a gift reserved solely for her daughters.

She was a real giver, her mother.

Her arms went around Sam's waist, and he got the bosom treatment. His cheeks were flushed when her mom let him up for air. "It's good to see you, Mrs. Donovan—"

"Jenny, please." She tittered. "Mrs. Donovan makes me feel old."

"Jenny," Sam said. "It's been a long time. How are you?"

Haley winced, and that time it wasn't because of her injuries. Both she and Sam had been out of the game too long if they were making a rookie mistake like asking her mom that question.

As predicted, that question continued the rant, but instead of plunking himself onto the couch and listening in abject horror as the tirade continued, Sam made his way into the kitchen and began putting away groceries. Her mother trailed him like a puppy, talking a mile a minute as he began rustling through bags.

"And then Haley didn't even call me to tell me she was okay." Another wail.

Good God, but how was her father still married to her mother?

Probably because he traveled most of the year.

Snorting, she maneuvered herself back onto her scooter and wheeled her way into the kitchen. Her mother's voice was nails on the chalkboard, but Sam didn't seem to mind as he puttered around.

"And I didn't sleep a wink," her mom said. "I'm so exhausted I can barely keep my eyes open."

One second Sam had been putting the milk away in the fridge, the next he was a flurry of movement and words. "Oh, I'm so sorry to hear that," he said, hustling over to lace his arm with her mother's. "You should go home *right now* and get some rest." He tugged her toward the front door and then out on to the porch.

"Oh no, I couldn't leave her—"

"I insist, Jenny," Sam said, and their voices faded until Haley heard her mom's car engine start and gravel kick up.

She leaned her head to the side, peering through the window as her mother's car disappeared down the road.

Sam walked back into the house, one last bag slung over his arm. "I bought these before I realized I'd unleashed your mother," he said, crossing over to her and pulling out a colorful bouquet of daffodils, sunflowers, and tulips. He set it on the counter in front of her before extracting a palm-sized teddy bear from the bag.

It was purple—her favorite color—and sporting a mournful expression as it clutched a tiny pillow embroidered with "I'm sorry."

"I would have bought you the giant one," he said, plunking it into her palm, "if I'd known that I'd unleashed the famous Mrs. Donovan tirade on you."

Haley glared at him.

She could not be bought with some weeds and a sad-looking stuffed toy. "Apology not accepted."

His lips twitched, totally unaffected by her show of temper. "You always could hold a grudge."

A huff as she crossed her arms. "Well, considering *you* hit *me* and thus unleashed the wrath of Jenny Donovan, I think this particular grudge is warranted."

"Maybe." He tugged on the end of her ponytail. "But one could also say that *technically* you're not supposed to slam on the brakes to avoid hitting an animal."

"Yeah," she muttered. "*You* tell that to Bambi."

Sam burst into laughter. "God, you could always make me laugh." His fingers came up to brush her cheek. "I really am—"

"Not allowed to apologize again."

His eyes warmed even as his laughter faded. It took every bit of her restraint to not lean into his touch, to not stretch up on her tiptoes—*tiptoe,* rather—and press her mouth to his.

She wanted to feel that warmth inside her, to wrap herself in him, not just physically, but in all the emotions he evoked in her.

She wanted . . . him.

God. A decade had passed, and she still felt the same damn way.

She was pathetic.

"Haley."

One terse word, but *oh* how she loved the sound of her name sliding across his tongue.

She forced her gaze from his lips, from the mouth she'd imagined slanting across hers so many times before. His eyes, an intoxicating mix of brown and green and gold, locked with hers, but this time there was something different in their depths.

Not pity or derision, which she half-expected, given that she *had* spent the last ten years mooning over him.

Nor was it confusion.

"Haley," he said again. Lower. Huskier.

Could it . . . *might* it be heat?

That notion didn't compute in her brain.

Sam had never looked at her like *that* before—with aware-ness, with desire. His palm slid across her cheek, tangling in the hair on her nape.

"Haley."

A benediction? A prayer for . . . forgiveness?

His head lowered and—

Was this really fucking happening?

Sam kissed her.

EIGHT

Sam

He was losing his mind.

He could not be kissing Haley.

Could. Not.

Except he was.

And it was fucking incredible.

She was broken and stitched up and probably concussed, and Haley's kiss was still the best of his life.

He tore his lips from hers. "I'm—"

She clamped a hand over his mouth, and considering it still held the teddy bear he'd bought her, Sam basically ate fur.

But her words had him forgetting that fact.

"You are not allowed to fucking apologize," she growled.

His fingers rose to extract the bear from Haley's grip—and his mouth. He set it on the counter, then removed a few stray hairs from the corners of his lips. The fuzzy stuffed toy might have been cute, but it definitely wasn't edible.

"Not *allowed?*" he asked.

"No," she said. "I've been dreaming about kissing you for—"

Horror crept into her expression, and this time she clamped a hand over her own mouth rather than his.

He bent slightly, locked his gaze onto hers. "For what?"

"No," she said. "I'm not doing this." Haley pushed herself backward, the wheels of the scooter skittering against the hardwood floor as she rounded the corner of the kitchen island and attempted to escape back down the hall.

Nope. No way. No how.

But though she had wheels, he was faster . . . and had two working legs.

He slipped in front of her.

"Not a word, Sam," she snapped. "I took a pain pill, and I'm a lightweight, and that means I'm going to start blabbering about how I've dreamed about kissing you since I was thirteen, and that it was even better in real life than in my dreams."

Silence. His. Of the stunned variety. As in, he had been stunned into muteness because . . . she'd liked him for more than a decade?

"Haley," he began.

She'd pressed her hands over her mouth again, cheeks bright pink, tears flooding those beautiful blue eyes, but in response to her name, she just shook her head.

"Sweetheart," he said, gentler.

Her lids slid closed.

"A decade?"

Another shake.

"Since Maggie?"

She swallowed hard.

He took a step toward her, reaching for her, wanting to haul her close and hold her until she realized that she had nothing to be embarrassed about, that childhood crushes weren't a big deal.

But the moment his fingers brushed her shoulder, Sam watched her eyes flash open, saw them fill with agony.

Because he was there. Because he was pushing this.

Hadn't he already done enough to her?

So, he stopped himself, forced his hands to drop back down to his sides. "I'll finish with the groceries," he said and turned back toward the kitchen, leaving Haley alone in the hall.

It was the absolute last thing he wanted to do.

But Sam did it anyway.

Forcing himself to walk away instead of fighting for what he wanted . . . well, that had become his specialty over the years.

Really, in the grand scheme of things, what was one more time?

SAM DIDN'T KNOW why he was still in Haley's kitchen.

He'd stashed the groceries, wiped the counters, straightened the bookcase, even alphabetized her now-antique DVD collection.

And she'd stayed in her bedroom.

All signs pointed for him to get the fuck out and yet . . . he couldn't.

She'd tasted like mint toothpaste, smelled like roses, felt like the softest silk . . . but sensations aside, he couldn't stop thinking about her revelation. Haley had liked him for years.

How? *Why?*

Perhaps more importantly, how hadn't he known?

Sure, they'd hung out a fair amount during his time with Maggie, but he'd never glimpsed one iota of a schoolgirl's crush from Haley. She'd been confident, self-assured and very busy with her own life.

To say his mind was blown would be the mother of all understatements.

Then he wondered if Maggie had known.

Hmm.

And why would it matter if she did? If Maggie *had* mentioned Haley's feelings to him, it wouldn't have changed anything, only served to make things uncomfortable for both him *and* Haley.

Maggie didn't like to make anyone feel uncomfortable.

Which had ultimately led to the demise of their relationship.

Sighing, he strode to the notepad in the kitchen, intending to leave Haley a note. He would go and check on her car, make sure it had been towed to the body shop as promised the previous night, maybe they could have a look at his door, and—

Crash.

Sam took off running before he'd even fully processed the noise.

He raced down the hall, into the bedroom, and found it empty. Spinning, he pushed open the door to the bathroom.

Haley was sprawled across the tile, and she was—

He averted his eyes.

Because she was naked.

She shrieked when she saw he'd come in. "Don't—*Sam!*" He'd dropped his eyes, just to confirm that she was, indeed, naked. And she *was*. So gloriously, sexily, *beautifully* naked that his cock twitched. Swallowing, he forced himself to focus, reaching for a towel and covering up the pertinent bits, even though he'd really been enjoying his view.

"What happened?"

Haley dropped her chin to her chest. "What do you think happened?"

"I *think* you were freaking out about something you didn't

need to, and so you decided to do something you weren't ready for." He used one finger to tip her chin back up, enough that those pretty blue eyes met his. "Didn't you just tell me you were a lightweight with the pain pills? As a nurse, what kind of symptoms do patients have when taking these kinds of medications?"

She crossed her arms, tucking the towel more firmly across herself.

"I can tell you that my four- and two-legged friends often experience lethargy and dizziness." He raised a brow. "Sound familiar?"

Haley sighed. "I'm fine. I literally fell from like six inches. I bent over to look for a bag in the cabinet and got lightheaded."

He gave a quick once-over of the parts he could see and, deciding that she'd told him the truth, reached behind her to turn on the taps. "You couldn't ask for help?"

Her bottom lip poked out. "I just wanted a bath, okay?" Another sigh. "Plus, I thought you'd gone."

"Why would you think that?" He tested the temperature then plugged the tub.

A roll of her eyes. "Because I freaked out on you? Because I basically told you I've been mooning over you since middle school?"

Surprised that she'd just lay it out there after her earlier horror, he asked, "So, are we over the embarrassment now?"

"God, no," she scoffed. "But the cat's out of the bag now. I might as well own it."

He tried to hold back his smile, but Haley caught it anyway. "You're enjoying this, aren't you?"

"A man does like to be appreciated." He winked.

"Oh, my God."

Sam pulled open the cabinet door and surveyed the contents before holding up a plastic trash bag. "This should work." He slipped it over the cast and used the drawstring to secure it in place.

Haley gave him a grudging nod. "Thanks."

He stood, extended a hand. "Towel."

"What?" Her cheeks flared. "*No.*"

"I'm not going to look. I'm just going to help you into the tub. The towel will be in the way."

Narrowed lids. "So, this isn't an excuse to see me naked?"

"I *already* saw you naked, remember? It's definitely—" He'd started to waggle his brows like a dirty old man but stopped when Haley sucked in a breath. Her face paled, and her eyes shimmered . . . with tears? "An excuse to see you naked," he finished lamely.

Um, what the hell was that?

"Oh," she replied softly. Her throat worked, and her lips pressed flat. "That's not what I thought—" Her gaze flicked to the tub. "Can you help me into the bath now?"

"Sure." Sam kept his stare firmly on her face as she shifted the towel aside, trying to puzzle out what the hell was going through that brain of hers.

Had he said something—?

No. Brian. It had to be.

Fucking asshole.

"Sam?" she asked.

He blinked. "Right." Carefully, he slid his arms underneath her, attempting to ignore the silkiness of her skin, the curves pressed against him. "You're beautiful," he told her as he maneuvered her into the water, thoroughly soaking himself in the process.

"Sam."

His arms were still under her, his chest rubbing against hers, his sodden T-shirt the only thing separating their naked skin.

"I don't know what that prick said to you," he said. "But you're gorgeous, sweetheart."

She shook her head and whether it was in response to him calling her gorgeous or a denial of the prick's statements, Sam didn't know.

Life was odd sometimes.

A person could go thirty-odd years ignoring or, maybe not noticing was a more accurate description, someone, and then boom, one moment—one collision, one *fucking* deer—and everything shifted.

Everything changed and morphed and rotated until the person that had always been categorized in a certain way, changed.

Until that one person who'd been on the periphery became firmly planted front and center.

He'd known Haley.

He'd respected her, thought she was funny and sweet and a really cool person.

But he hadn't wanted her, hadn't noticed her eyes, her lips, her body.

Then *wham*, the pieces had come together, and he was left wondering how he could have missed her all along.

Sam tilted his head, lifting his mouth so he could whisper in her ear. "You're the most beautiful woman I've ever seen." When she opened her mouth, no doubt to deny his words, he leaned back and snapped. "*No.*"

Her eyes went wide.

"I know the timing was wrong before—we were teenagers and I was with Maggie. But I was an idiot to not notice how much you'd changed when you came back into town last year. Yes, your body is hot, sweetheart, but it's what's in here"—he tapped the spot above his heart—"that is truly beautiful."

"I've seen you at the hospital with patients. I've seen you

with your nieces and nephews and your friends." He cupped her cheek. "On the inside, where it *really* matters, you're a good person."

She bit her lip, making him want to kiss her all over again.

But it wasn't the right time.

"Brian was a fucking idiot to betray you."

She blinked rapidly.

"But I think . . ." He trailed off.

"You think?" she asked softly.

"I think his loss might be my gain."

NINE

Haley

Uн. *What?*

Another brush of Sam's fingers across her jaw before he straightened and turned to leave the bathroom. "No more shenanigans," he said, pausing on the threshold. "Holler for me when you're done."

And he walked out, shutting the door behind him.

"I—" She shook her head, looking around the room, half expecting the tile walls to provide her with an answer.

Sam thought she was beautiful. Inside and out.

What in the what?

It wasn't like she thought she was an ugly or even a bad person, but she could freely admit that her confidence had taken a hit after Brian. But then again what person was cheated on and *didn't* internalize the other person's actions? What person didn't take them as a blow to their self-worth?

Well, if she ever met another person who continued on with

their life all fine and dandy and untouched by such a betrayal, then she'd be sure to ask them their secret.

Because Brian had screwed with her head.

Yes, he'd cheated, and that was bad enough.

But he'd also managed to drill down into her deep, vulnerable underbelly even before she'd discovered the affair. First, it was little comments here or there—stating how she needed to pick up another workout so she could be *healthy* for the wedding. Later, it became adopting a diet because her clothes didn't fit as well as they used to. Then it was dyeing her hair because she had gray showing. Or expensive wrinkle cream because she had fine lines developing on her forehead and around her eyes.

If he'd led with wrinkle cream, she would have told him to fuck off, but Brian hadn't. Instead, he'd slowly and persistently undermined her sense of self.

He managed to pinpoint all her insecurities—yes, she'd been twenty-five and getting gray, yes, she had laugh lines, yes, she'd put on a few pounds—and then just amplified each one by a thousand.

Add that in with the stress of working in a very busy emergency department in a very busy hospital and suddenly, she'd become a ball of nerves.

Doubting herself. Doubting her abilities.

"Ugh," she muttered, sliding down into the tub so her shoulders were under the warm water. Her cast clanged against the cast iron, but firmly encased in her post-pain-pill glory, Haley felt no pain.

The bathroom door cracked. "Please, tell me that wasn't your head," Sam said.

Despite herself, she grinned. "Not my head."

"Good." The wood panel started to close.

"Wait."

It paused.

"Thanks for helping me," she said into the little black line. "For staying."

"I'm here, Haley." The door started moving again, sliding against the frame but just before the latch clicked shut, she heard: "However long you need me."

Her eyes closed, and she leaned her head back against the lip. "But for how long though?" she whispered. Because sooner or later this bubble surrounding them would burst. Sam would go back to work at his clinic, she to the hospital. She'd be the little sister again, the amusing sibling of the girl he'd once almost married.

He'd go back to his world, and she'd go back to hers . . . only this time she would know exactly what it felt like to kiss him.

SAM POKED his head back into the bathroom just as Haley was dozing off.

Probably a good thing because she really didn't need to add a near-drowning to her concussion and broken leg.

Though, her head was starting to clear up.

Or maybe that was just the pain medication wearing off since her ankle had decided it needed to play an orchestra of aches and throbs and zings in concert up her leg.

"You're hurting," Sam said, holding up a towel and keeping his eyes locked on hers.

Not on her body. He was behaving all gentleman-like.

It was just too bad that she didn't want him to be a gentleman.

"I'm fine," she said, rubbing her pulsing temple.

He pulled the plug on the tub. "You're not fine," he said. "Besides your head, what's hurting?"

"Is this what you do?" she muttered. "Corner naked women in bathtubs until they reveal all of their secrets?"

"Is it working?"

She took the towel when he extended it in her direction, holding it above her torso until the water drained enough for her to drape it over herself. "No."

"Damn."

A twitch of lips that reminded her exactly how they'd felt *twitching* against hers.

The man was a menace.

Also. Concussion. *That* was why she was losing her mind. It was the only explanation for why her body had decided that despite the stitches and broken bones, she wanted him.

"What just went through your head?" he asked.

Yeah, no. Nice try. That was a fun fact she definitely *wasn't* sharing.

Snorting, Haley let him help her up to sitting. "Wouldn't you like to know?"

"I would," he replied, wrapping the towel more securely around her upper body. "Hence, the reason I asked."

He bent close and slid his arms around her and—*fuck*—but she liked that.

Except . . . she *couldn't* like that.

"So?" he asked, pausing there, somehow both too close and not close enough.

"So what?" She played dumb.

He snorted, brushed a lock of hair off her cheek. "What went through your brain?"

A sigh. "Nothing," she muttered, closing her eyes. Exhaustion pulled at her, making her mind fuzzy, her thoughts spinning around her brain like snow flurries.

Sam pressed his lips to her forehead, making her lids fly open.

His eyes were on hers, his mouth *oh so close.* She wanted it against hers again, she wanted to see if the second touch of his lips could top the first. But why had he stayed? Was it guilt because she'd been hurt, or could it maybe be . . . attraction?

Ha. His sweet sentiments aside, that wasn't even in the realm of possibilities.

And so, she doubled down. "Nothing went through my head."

"Lie," he said. "But I'm not going to pressure a concussed woman any further."

Despite the kiss—because clearly, that was due to adrenaline at having successfully avoided a patented Mrs. Donovan tirade or guilt or hell, maybe *he* was mildly concussed—because she *knew* that Sam couldn't be attracted to her.

First, he was way out of her league.

Second, she'd admitted to a long-held crush, which was pretty much a ten-out-of-ten on the How Pathetic and/or Crazy Is She scale?

Third, and probably most important, he'd broken Maggie's heart.

Her sister was the one person in her life who'd always been there for her, and Sam had hurt her. It didn't matter that things between them seemed okay now. The end of their relationship had destroyed Maggie, and even putting aside the fact that Sam could just as easily do the same to her, Haley knew she could never be with someone who'd so thoroughly wounded her sister.

Nope. Not going to happen.

Even if he was an excellent kisser.

Really, that was *not* the point.

Sam wrapped his arms tighter around her and tugged her against his chest. Her heart fluttered, and she started to protest. "I can—"

"Shush," he said, cradling her close and standing. "I've got you."

Haley would have loved to blame her lack of further objection on her spinning head, or her aching leg, or the sudden, overwhelming fatigue enveloping her, but the truth was that being held so carefully, assured so confidently, felt . . . incredible.

He had her.

Yet, it all meant nothing, she reminded herself. It was a random kiss, the comforting words of an old friend, a gentle embrace for someone who was hurting.

That was it.

But as he helped her slip fresh pajamas on and tucked her into bed then brought her a bowl filled with banana ice cream, she wondered.

Was it *really* nothing?

Or could it possibly be the start of something more?

Nothing, she thought determinedly, after he'd taken the bowl back to the kitchen and she couldn't keep her eyes open any longer. *Definitely nothing.*

TEN

Sam

ANOTHER NIGHT. Another couch.

Or rather, another night, the *same* couch.

Sam had run home for a change of clothes while Haley was sleeping then had thrown together a simple meal of pasta and salad for dinner once he'd returned to Haley's house. He'd gone to wake her for the meal, but she'd been sleeping so deeply that he had decided to leave her be.

Her body needed the rest.

So, he had wrapped up a plate and left it in her fridge and then debated whether to go home or to stay.

Ultimately, he decided to stay again in case she needed him.

Didn't he mean, in case she got dizzy from the medication again?

No. He meant, in case she needed *him*.

Probably going to be a problem, but not one he was actively avoiding, especially when his phone pinged and he saw a text from Maggie.

It was just after dinnertime, and he knew that meant Sunday Donovan dinner had likely just finished. He *also* knew the meal had probably included a discussion of his appearance at Haley's house that morning.

Bracing himself, he opened the message.

Samwise. I don't know if I should hunt you down and slice you into tiny little pieces because you hurt my sister or thank you because you saved her from our mother.

God, that fucking nickname. Just because a guy had liked *Lord of the Rings* once upon a time. *But* he'd known Maggie for plenty long enough, and two could play that game.

Maggie-baggie. I expected you to show up and save the day.

A pause. Then:

One, I'd almost blocked that horrible nickname from memory. Two, that's why I'm texting. Is Haley doing okay? Lane is sick and Tim is out of town, so my mom decided to bring dinner to me. I couldn't get away until now, and Haley isn't replying to my texts.

Sam considered the question then figured he might as well answer it truthfully. Haley was beautiful and funny, and he wanted to get to know her as . . . well, an adult. Which made him sound like a total creep, but he'd been friends with the girl. The woman was a completely different mystery that he wanted to solve.

Did he want to be her friend? Yes, definitely.

But he also wanted more. He wanted to know her as a man knows a woman he cares about. Not platonically.

"Fuck," he muttered. Why was he beating around the bush? He was attracted to Haley. He liked her. He *wanted* her.

Big fucking deal.

Except—his phone buzzed again, reminding him that things weren't that simple. That he and Haley had history.

Sighing, he saw the follow-up question mark Maggie had sent. Then girded his loins and replied.

> *That nickname is a classic (and remember I have more before you pull out Samwise again). But nicknames aside, Haley's fine. I just checked on her a few minutes ago and she's sleeping. I stocked her fridge, am parked on her couch, and can keep an eye on her tonight. But tomorrow I have a full day and she could use some supervision. The pain medication makes her dizzy.*

The " . . . " signaling the start of Maggie's reply began almost immediately. Then stopped. Then started again.

And one more stop.

Finally, Sam put Maggie out of her misery and just called her.

"Sam Johnson, you're sleeping with my sister?" she hissed.

He sighed. "Stop and rethink that statement," he told her. "Because that sounded like a Jenny Donovan special. I'm staying on your sister's couch because she's alone and aside from the broken leg, stitches, and concussion, her medication makes her dizzy."

"Oh."

He leaned back against the cushions. "Yeah, *oh.*"

"I wonder why Brian didn't fly out."

Sam sucked in a breath. He wasn't touching that with a ten-foot pole.

"What the hell does that mean?" Maggie demanded.

Shit. He'd been with this woman for six years. She *knew* him, and she definitely knew when he was lying. Still, Sam tried to play it cool. "Me breathing?"

"No, not you breathing, you idiot," Maggie snapped. "What do you know about Brian and Haley?"

"Nothing," he said, thinking the idiot comment was probably well-earned. For as much as she knew him, he also knew her. And when Maggie got something in her head, she was a dog to a bone.

In these cases, it was best to divert and avoid.

"Sam."

He closed his eyes. "Maggie." A beat. "I'm hanging up now."

"Sam—"

"Goodbye, Maggie," he said. "I've got to be out at Roosevelt Ranch early in the morning. Make sure you check on your sister."

"Don't you—"

He hung up and sighed loudly.

Which is probably why he missed the sound of Haley's little scooter. "I didn't know you were on chatting terms with my sister."

Sam's eyes flew open.

His gaze traveled over her face. Her color was closer to normal, and there were no signs of strain around her mouth and eyes. "You're feeling better."

She was beautiful, even with the bandage marring her forehead, curls of black and purple creeping from beneath it and spreading across her forehead.

One half of her mouth curved up. "How do you always know?"

He shrugged and pushed up off the couch. "My patients can't talk to me." Pointing to the couch, he said, "Means I have to be observant. Now, sit. I'll heat up your plate."

"Plate?" Haley started to frown but paused midway and winced. Shaking her head, she shifted herself onto the couch. "You didn't have to cook for me, Sam. Hell, you shouldn't even be here. You've got your own job and your own life, and just because you're feeling guilty"—she pointed a finger at him —"and you *shouldn't* even be feeling guilty at all because I was the one who slammed on my brakes, remember? But just because you are doesn't mean that you should put everything that's happening in your own life on hold."

He had been waiting for a pause in her speech. "You done?"

Her gaze narrowed. "You going to be a pain in my ass?"

"Probably." He grinned. "But it's not going to stop me. For one, my life is boring. I have work and . . . work. My friends are all married with kids, and my parents aren't even in town right now." When her brows drew down, he said, "They winter in Florida, like a pair of migrating birds."

Her mouth curved. "I'd forgotten they wanted to do that. Did they ever get the RV they wanted?"

Sam chuckled. "It's nicer than my house. They spend most of their time traveling around the States and will occasionally grace me with their presence by parking on my driveway for a week or two."

He tucked a pillow under Haley's foot. "Living the dream," she said.

"They have their own Instagram account." He tugged a blanket from the back of the couch and draped it over her. "Last week, I saw my mom had used the hashtag YOLO."

She snorted. "Cooler than me."

"Ditto that." He straightened and headed for the kitchen. "I just made some pasta and salad, you hungry?"

Considering her response was her stomach growling nearly loud enough to shake the foundation of her little cottage, Sam hustled to the fridge and pulled out her plate.

Just as he was popping it into the microwave, she said, loudly enough he couldn't ignore it, not with the open floorplan of her kitchen and living room, "So, Maggie?" she asked.

Sam stifled a sigh. He'd never discussed with Haley—hell, he'd never really discussed with anyone—why he'd broken off his engagement with Haley's sister. That was between him and Maggie, and they'd made their peace when he'd moved back to Darlington to take over the veterinary practice three years before.

"Maggie and I talk on occasion." She was married with kids and happy. That was all that mattered to him now.

Sam pulled out the bowl of salad and brought it and a fork over to Haley.

"Really?" she asked as he handed it to her. "That's all you're going to say?"

"Would you like me to press you for more details of what happened with Brian? Especially since your sister apparently doesn't know you two broke up."

Haley speared a forkful of spinach. "No one knows we broke up except him and me, and well, *you*. Though I guess Susie knows, too." She jammed the spinach into her mouth.

"Susie your friend?" he asked.

"Uh-huh," she said around the bite before swallowing. "Though *former* friend is a better description. And I didn't deliberately not tell anyone we'd broken up. I just didn't go out of my way to . . . *tell* them."

"You've been back how long exactly?"

A cough trailed by a mumbled answer.

"Sorry?" He put his hand to his ear. "What was that?"

She made a face. "Thirteen months."

"Ah. That's what my Haley translator missed. Thirteen months is a long time to keep up the charade of a relationship."

"It's not a charade," she protested and shoved another bite into her mouth.

"Then what is it?" he pressed.

She chewed. Swallowed. "It's a—"

The microwave dinged.

He laughed. "Look at that. The universe is giving you time to come up with an answer." He started to walk back into the kitchen, but she stopped him with a hand on his arm.

"I don't need time," she said.

"I'm teasing you." Sam bent so that his eyes were in line with hers. "You don't owe me an answer."

Her expression warmed. "I know. But I think I might owe myself one."

ELEVEN

Haley

WHY WAS SHE PUSHING THIS?

Sam had given her the perfect out. An easy way to find some distance again and to avoid—

Well, she'd done entirely too much of *that* in her twenty-seven years.

"I didn't correct my mom or Maggie about Brian because"—she sucked in a breath—"I didn't want to deal with it. No." She shook her head. "That's not what I mean. I . . . just with me having a fiancé, things were easier, simpler. My mom didn't hassle me, Maggie backed off about trying to set me up with all of the single guys in town—"

She broke off.

Because that was what she'd been telling herself.

But what she'd been telling herself, the story she'd grasped on to tightly with both hands like when her niece, Ashley, had refused to let go of her blankie when she'd been a toddler, was absolutely and utterly an excuse.

She'd held on to Brian because—

"I didn't want to be pathetic."

He faced hardened. "You're *not*. That's ridic—"

"Don't say it's ridiculous," she said. "You're not in here"—she tapped her temple—"you're not in my brain. You don't know what it's like."

Sam froze. "So, what's it like?" He knelt in front of the couch, taking the bowl from her hands and setting it on the coffee table. "Tell me what's going on"—he gently touched one finger to her forehead—"in here."

She forced a laugh. "It's not a pretty sight."

"In the last twenty-four hours, we've done bruises, blood, and broken bones . . . I don't think we should be worried about things being pretty, do you?"

Her lips twitched. "Well, for starters, if you'd said that to me a year ago, I would have automatically assumed that you were saying *I* wasn't pretty."

"I—"

She waved a hand. "Yes, I know you didn't mean it that way at all. I just—I don't know, I guess I always have to fight the urge to immediately look for some hidden insult in someone else's words." Her chin wobbled. "It's stupid. Logically, I know that, but I still can't stop myself from digging for some buried slight. And I was like that *before* Brian."

He brushed his fingers over her cheek. "And after?"

"Being with him"—a long slow breath—"amplified every insecurity I've battled my whole life. Not thin and beautiful like Maggie. Not smart enough. Not perfect." Her voice dropped. "Unloveable."

Ugh. Haley blinked back tears and released another shuddering exhale.

Because, yes, she felt that way—or rather, she *had* felt that way.

But she'd grown since then. She understood herself better, knew she didn't have to be perfect, that she had value even if she was five pounds overweight or didn't automatically know the solution to a problem big or small.

Of course, that also didn't mean the echoes of those doubts were completely gone.

They framed every interaction, were a constant struggle to shrug off, to not internalize—

"That is such fucking bullshit."

Her jaw dropped open at his tone, but she didn't have a chance to respond because then his mouth was on hers. His lips were hard at first, almost angry because of what she'd admitted, but then they softened. His mouth gently coaxed hers, his tongue slipping between her lips, brushing against hers, tender and sweet and—

He pulled back. "I'm sorry. I didn't mean what *you* were saying was bullshit. Just that I hate you felt that way because you're gorgeous and smart and totally, utterly love—"

This time *she* kissed *him*.

There was no hesitation in his response. One second, he was mid-sentence, the next his mouth was firmly against hers and though he held her gently, Sam still managed to give her the hottest kiss of her life.

He nipped at her bottom lip and when she gasped, he slipped his tongue inside her mouth to tangle with hers. Calloused fingers slid over her nape, curled into her hair, angling her head so he could deepen the kiss.

Hot, a little rough, and so *fucking* good.

Haley pressed herself up, even as she yanked him down. She needed him closer, on top of her, *inside* of her. She—

A bolt of pain had her gasping . . . this time not in a good way.

Sam realized immediately, and he launched himself off her.

She'd managed to pull him partway onto the couch, and while that was what her vagina wanted—or rather it wanted more, starting with the rigid length of him that was nudging her thigh sliding home—the rest of her body was intrinsically aware that she'd been in an accident the night before.

Sam was big. *Ha.* Okay, he was heavy. There. *That* was a better descriptor, one that didn't bring her inner teenage boy roaring to life.

"I'm sorry, baby," he said. "I forgot—"

She smiled up at him, heart pounding, head spinning—in pleasure rather than because of the concussion—her lips tender and swollen. "I forgot, too," she said.

He cupped her cheek. "I meant what I said. You have worth, sweetheart. And that doesn't come because your outside is pretty—though it *is* gorgeous—but because you're a good person and so damned brilliant and . . ."

Keeping all the negative things inside her brain had meant she'd been giving them power. But somehow, the moment she'd verbalized those deep dark thoughts, the moment she'd admitted aloud how much the burden carrying all of that had been weighing on her, it was almost as if their power over her disappeared.

Haley could take Sam's words at face value instead of sifting through them for a backhanded compliment.

She could imagine a world, imagine herself in a world where a man like Sam actually believed the things he was saying.

She could be pretty and brilliant and *imperfect.*

And that was okay.

Shock weaved through her, chased rapidly by awe. She didn't *have* to be perfect. She could be herself and still be worthy.

Huh.

Fancy that.

TWELVE

Sam

HE WAS knee-deep in horse manure and loving every minute of it.

Ankle-deep might have been a more accurate description. Though his arm was in what most would consider a much worse place as he examined Kelly Hamilton's horse, Stella.

Kelly and her husband, Justin, owned Roosevelt Ranch, which was quickly becoming one of the premier breeding operations in the States. Kelly was also Rob's sister-in-law.

See? Darlington was a small town. They didn't even need six degrees of separation.

Still, despite Kel managing a breeding program, Sam had the notion *this* particular pregnancy wasn't planned.

"Is she okay?" Kelly asked nervously.

He nodded. "Yup."

Kelly blew out a relieved sigh as he finished his exam then took a few minutes to discard the glove and scrub his hands with soap and water in the nearby sink.

"So, do you have any idea why she's been so moody?"

"I'm guessing because she's about three months pregnant." He could have confirmed that more accurately if he'd brought his portable ultrasound, but apparently Kel had been adamant that Stella was not pregnant when she'd scheduled the appointment with Jane. "So, I'm guessing this isn't planned?"

Melissa, Kelly's sister and Rob's wife, chose that moment to walk through the door, two thermoses of coffee in her hands. She'd obviously overheard him because she grinned and teased, "Like mother, like daughter?"

Kel shot her a sisterly glare. "Things happen sometimes, okay?"

Melissa bumped her with her shoulder. "I'm teasing because, yes, sometimes things do happen . . . for the better."

Kelly's face softened and she snagged a thermos from her sister. "Thanks for the coffee."

"You're welcome." Melissa turned to Sam and extended the second thermos.

"Oh, no," he said, despite the mouth-watering smell of the freshly brewed drink wafting to his nose. "That's yours. I couldn't—"

"I already had mine. I made this for you when Kel told me you were coming to the ranch." She shoved the cup at him and since he wasn't about to let good coffee go to waste, Sam took it.

As he drank his first sip, she asked, "How are you? I heard you had an . . . eventful weekend."

He made a face that had Melissa tipping up the bottom of the thermos and dumping another sip into his mouth. "Drink," she said. "Everything is better with coffee."

Sam obeyed then nearly groaned in relief as the caffeine headed straight from his mouth to his brain.

Yup. That was just what he'd needed.

"Better?"

A nod.

"Now, you'll tell us what happened?"

"You probably know as much as I do," he said. "But Haley is pretty banged up. She has a broken ankle along with a concussion and stitches." As he listed her injuries, the guilt peppered him anew. If only he hadn't—

"More coffee," Melissa said.

"Go easy on the full Missy offensive," Kel interjected, sipping her own coffee and leaning back next to him against the closed door of Stella's stall. "The poor man has had a time of it."

"I hope you're not feeling guilty," Melissa said. "Rob told me that a deer jumped in front of Haley's car. It was just an—"

"Accident?" He met her eyes. "And how would *you* feel if someone was hurt because you hit their car?"

Melissa wrinkled her nose.

"Yeah," he said. "That."

"Okay, *I* may have a problem with guilt but . . ."

"Don't finish that sentence, Sissy," Kel warned. "Because it's all aboard the pot-meet-kettle train." She grinned when Melissa smacked her. "Let's talk about Stella instead."

Melissa's expression filled with glee. "Yes, let me tease you about your horse's unplanned pregnancy some more."

"You're so sweet to me." Kel pushed up and wrapped an arm around Melissa's shoulders. Or maybe it was her neck, he realized with a grin. "So supportive—"

"Your horse is a hussy."

A mock gasp. "How *dare* you . . ."

Sam couldn't hold back his chuckle, even as their squabbling made him jealous.

As an only child with parents constantly on the road, he'd had more than his fair share of loneliness over the last few years. Yes, he'd dated some, but no one had stuck, and so he'd developed a pattern of working long hours and then going home to his meal for one at the end of the night.

Which might be a little pathetic, but instead of going down that particular line of thinking, Sam was just going to pretend it was totally completely normal for a grown man to be alone and . . .

It wasn't like he was *all* alone.

He saw his clients—people like Melissa and Kelly and, even Snapchat Esther, who'd gotten a new kitten. He traveled to the nearby ranches, which he supposed could fall under the client section of his life. But he went into town a lot, grocery shopping or eating at Henry's diner when he needed to be around people.

Might be a teensy bit pathetic, that train of thought.

But pathetic or not, Sam couldn't smother the feeling that he'd been waiting.

For what, he wasn't sure.

At least, he *hadn't* been sure until he'd crashed into Haley. Because after the collision, after the time at her house, after the *kiss* . . . he wondered if he hadn't been waiting all along for Haley.

"So, if Stella is such a virginal being," Melissa said, tugging Kel's arm from around her neck, "then how is she knocked up?"

"Immaculate horse-ception?" Sam deadpanned, earning him a smack from Kelly.

"Shut it you." Kel tapped her finger to her mouth. "But yours is a good question, sissy."

"What's a good question?" They all turned to see Justin striding into the barn, his and Kelly's daughter, Abigail, riding on his shoulders.

"Stella's pregnant," Kelly said.

"What?" Justin asked, sliding closer to Stella's stall when Abigail said, "Swella!" and leaned forward, nearly toppling herself from his hold.

"I've got you, sweetie pie," Kelly said, swooping in and hugging Abigail to her chest. "Do you want to see Stella?"

The little girl smiled. "Yes."

Kelly lifted her up so she could pet the front of Stella's head. "The twins?" she asked.

"Still sleeping," he said and held up a baby monitor. "Just this one"—he smacked a kiss to the top of Abigail's head—"that decided she was raring to start her Monday."

"Don't know where she gets the energy," Kelly said.

Justin waggled his brows. "I know."

"Barf," Melissa said, her eyes dancing.

Kel's lips twitched. "Why do I feel like you've been waiting years to say that?"

Melissa grinned. "Because considering the number of times you've said it about me and my husband, I definitely have been waiting to turn the tables."

"Terrible."

Melissa blew her a kiss. "You love me." She pulled out her phone, glanced at its screen. "Well, I just wanted to drop by and make sure everything was good with your first baby," she told Kel. "But it looks like Rob is sending out the S.O.S. to get the kiddos ready for school."

"Stella's not my first baby," Kel said then frowned. "Okay, fine, she basically is, but knowing you with your *own* babies, you've got the schedule down to the second and everything already laid out. Rob just needs to follow the plan."

A shrug. "Of course, I do." She grinned as her phone buzzed again. "It's just that plans tend to go out the window when Allie decides she doesn't want to wear any pants."

It was Justin's turn to frown as he voiced the same question Sam was thinking. "Can't she just wear a dress?"

Melissa smirked, patting him on the cheek. "Oh, you poor, poor dear. Just wait until that one"—she pointed at Abigail

—"gets bigger. My daughter has decided that pants, shorts, sweats, skirts, dresses, *and* underwear are all too restrictive. She wants to be completely bottomless all the time."

Sam made a strangled noise.

Melissa's eyes flicked to his. "Case in point, Rob's reaction." She held up the phone so they could all see the screen and the GIF Rob had sent of an actor running around a room screaming.

They all shared a laugh as she hugged each of them in turn and then said goodbye.

Sam figured it was time for him to make an exit as well.

If he hurried, he might have a chance to check on Haley before he headed into the clinic.

"I'll swing by next week with my ultrasound and we'll see if we can find out exactly how far along she is," he said, gathering up his supplies and tucking them back into his kit.

"What I still don't understand is how she's pregnant in the first place," Kelly said, having set down Abigail and moved to the table to cut up an apple. She helped her daughter feed a slice to each of the horses one by one. "We've been so careful to keep the horses separate while they're in season and—"

Sam caught Justin's wince at the same time Kelly did.

"Justin Roosevelt," she began, thunder in her tone. "What *did* you do?"

He winced and held up the baby monitor. "Oh look, the twins—"

"That isn't even on," Kelly snapped, yanking it from his hand and twisting the volume dial. A picture filled the screen, showing two sleeping babies, each in their own crib.

"I should go—"

They didn't acknowledge him, so Sam began to make his escape.

He was at the barn door when he heard Justin confess, "So, like a month ago, remember you and Melissa took the girls to

Disney on Ice? The twins were, well, *the twins,* and I may have forgotten Stella was in heat when I turned her and Theo out to pasture together."

Kelly gasped. "You forgot?"

Sam started to close the door behind him, figuring to give them some privacy for their argument, but when he turned to do so, he saw Justin had tugged Kelly close.

He should look away. He really should.

But instead, Sam found himself riveted.

"Admit it," he said. "You're not really mad."

She huffed, turned her head away, but not before Sam saw that she was smiling. "I get to keep the baby?"

Justin kissed her forehead, glancing over to check on Abigail who was practicing her saddling skills on a kid-sized stuffed horse. "As if we could ever give a Stello baby up."

"Stello?" Abby asked.

"Theo and Stella," Justin said as if it were obvious. "I've been coming up with combo names ever since I saw Theo mounting Stella and giving her his—"

Kel gave an outraged gasp. "Don't talk about her that way—"

Justin cut off the rest of her protest by kissing her.

Sam figured *that* was definitely his cue and tugged the barn door closed.

A few minutes later, he drove to Haley's house and couldn't stop the longing from swarming over him. He wanted what Jordan and Kelly had, what Melissa and Rob also had—easy, comfortable, teasing, even a little irritated . . .

But love.

All of it was love.

Sam wanted that.

And he thought he might want it with Haley.

THIRTEEN

Haley

It had been five days, and Haley was losing her fucking mind.

No work. No car—hers was in the shop with a wish and a prayer the mechanic could make it drivable again, not that she could drive anyway, considering her right ankle was the one she'd broken. She'd binged as many reality TV shows and documentaries as she could handle and had far exceeded her e-book budget for the month. She had even progressed beyond just talking to herself.

Now she was arguing with herself.

"No, you can't," she muttered as she considered crutching her butt out into her backyard for some fresh air and change of location. "Yes, I can." She hadn't needed any pain pills that day, so there was no risk of being too dizzy and cracking her head open.

But, she probably shouldn't.

The skies had opened up that morning, dumping buckets of

rain onto Darlington and turning her yard into a giant mud pit.

"Fuck it," she said. "I'm going."

She tucked her crutches under her armpits and thumped herself to the back door. Her scooter was useless on the steps and just as much so on the uneven path weaving its way through her garden. Mother Nature might have wreaked havoc in her yard, but Haley couldn't deal with being sedentary any longer. She was used to moving, to being on her feet and running around the hospital for twelve hours at a time, not propping herself in front of her TV and her only exercise being when she wheeled herself down the hall to the toilet.

She needed to find a way to get back to work, even if it was just for charting or to answer phones.

Being here, alone, except for her sister's daily visit, meant she was going crazy.

Her sister had visited. Not Sam.

"So, he missed one day," she reminded herself. "He was probably busy with work and—"

He'd forgotten about her.

Haley wrinkled her nose. He *hadn't* forgotten about her. Sam had been by every morning and every evening. He hadn't stayed on her couch again, though she considered that a good sign, as in she had recovered enough from her injuries that she didn't need a babysitter.

Her concussion symptoms—mild to begin with—had all but faded. Her ankle still ached, and she was weeks away from being able to bear weight on it, let alone driving.

And Sam hadn't come that morning.

Or that night.

The sun was setting, and Haley had reheated the pasta he'd made for them the previous night for dinner. The man could cook—though to be fair to chefs everywhere, it *was* limited to one solid meal. As she'd waited for him to appear, she'd considered calling him to say thanks for the yummy leftovers, but one, she didn't have Sam's number and two, she wasn't sure she had the right to call him even if she did.

And . . . he hadn't come.

Which meant she was slowly, incrementally going insane.

Should she call Maggie for his number? Obviously, her sister and Sam talked regularly. But what would Maggie think or assume or pinpoint with laser-like accuracy?

That Haley liked Sam? That she missed him? That her sister was trying to horn in on her ex?

Sighing, she crutched a few steps farther down the path before carefully lowering herself to a dry spot, or rather, a space that was damp but not thoroughly soaked.

The evening air had a bite to it, just enough to make the end of her nose and the tops of her cheeks tingle. Rain aside, it really had been a beautiful spring week. Warm, but not the scorching heat of summer. No snow, no ice.

And she was hobbled by her broken ankle.

"Lame," she muttered, leaning back against a rock and staring up at the sky. The sun had technically already set, the evening entering its twilight state as its shadows began to swallow the sunlight, dark bleaching the colorful flowers of her yard to different shades of gray.

Yet, the moon was bright and full and beautiful, and a few stars were beginning to appear on the darkening curve of the sky, royal to navy to black. She reclined against the rock and just watched as day turned fully to night.

The moon, shining brightly and yet so alone was lovely in its own way, but its isolation did nothing to dispel the loneliness within her.

Sam owed her nothing . . . and he'd somehow still become an addiction.

Five days, apparently, was all it took.

She snorted. Because she knew it hadn't been five days, not this boy she'd crushed on for so long. *But* in those five days, Haley had grown to really like the man, and she wanted to know him further.

A dangerous thought considering what had happened with Maggie.

Also, one she hadn't been able to get out of her mind, despite the past, despite her misgivings, despite her sister.

"Ugh," she said, knowing she was twisting herself into knots for no reason.

Sam hadn't expressed any interest—

Cough. The kisses?

See what she meant about arguing with herself?

Yes, he'd kissed her.

Twice. *No,* three times.

Yes, it had been three times. But that had been on Sunday and it was Friday now, and he had been over eight times since the kiss—*kisses*—and . . . he hadn't tried to kiss her again.

In fact, he hadn't been anything aside from friendly.

No flirting. No searing eye contact. No gentle caresses and . . . no kisses.

She'd been friend-zoned.

Hence the late-night garden brooding.

Haley sighed, thus confirming said brooding. Sam had said all the right things, made her feel better, made sure she was healing and settled.

He'd done *everything* right.

But for a second there, she'd thought that maybe, just maybe she might have a chance at getting her mess of a love life straightened out. Because Sam was sweet and kind and hot and sexy and—

He wasn't for her.

"Yeah," she said, adding another broody sigh, just for good measure. "I need to remember that."

"Remember what?"

Sam's voice made her gasp.

But before she could scramble to come up with a response, the clouds she'd noticed but hadn't particularly processed as dark or storm-wielding, opened up and rain poured down across her backyard for the second time that day.

"Shit," she cried, reaching for her crutches and fumbling to get herself up onto her feet.

"Let me." Sam scooped her up into his arms. He stood, running to the back porch and depositing her beneath the cover, before returning for her crutches. After tucking them inside her back door, he swept back over to her, gathering her against his chest again and carrying her inside.

They were both soaked to the skin. Rivulets of icy water pooled in her hair, dripping down her nape, her face. Despite the cold, Sam was somehow still hot, his body heat almost scorching her through the layers of their wet clothes.

"Wait here," he said, setting her on the kitchen counter and hustling down the hall.

A heartbeat later he was back, setting a towel around her shoulders then wrapping one above her cast to catch the water.

Smart man. Brilliant man. Sweet man.

"Sam—"

He glanced up, and her breath caught at the heat in his eyes. "You okay?" he asked.

Where had all the reasons to give this man a wide berth disappeared to?

Because in *that* moment, his brown hair darkened to black, water dripping down his forehead, his cheeks, his mouth, his wet clothes sticking to a muscled chest, to thighs she wanted pressing against hers . . . *fuck*, she wanted nothing more than to reach up and slant her mouth across his.

He was staring at her as though he wanted her.

For a moment, she could actually believe it.

Sam cleared his throat, the heat disappeared. "Let me get you some dry clothes."

Haley lifted her hand, placed it on his shoulder when he would have turned away. "Wait."

"You—?"

She kissed him.

If he'd had a heartbeat of hesitation or resistance or any type of shock that her twisted mind might have interpreted as not wanting the kiss—not wanting *her*—Haley might have shut down.

But there wasn't any hesitation in Sam's reaction.

The moment her lips pressed to his, he was a flurry of motion. One hand came up to weave into her hair, his tongue slid through the seam of her mouth, slipping inside to tangle with hers. The other arm wrapped tightly around her middle, crushing her against all the long, lean muscle she'd been admiring only seconds before.

And it felt . . . right.

Also incredible, of course. He was hot as hell, and he was kissing her with so much intensity that her mind spun.

But it wasn't just heat, definitely wasn't solely desire.

This man kissed her, and the rest of the world fell away.

His fingers slipped under the hem of her T-shirt, sliding up her rib cage, leaving a trail of goose bumps in their wake.

She moaned, wrapped her uninjured leg around his hips. "Fuck." A gasp as she felt the hard length of him against her pussy. She wanted both of their pants off. Now. Then his fingers teased the underside of her breasts and she arched, wanting it all, wanting him inside, wanting his hand to move higher, to slip under her bra. "*Sam*," she pleaded.

He nipped her jaw, soothed the slight hurt with his tongue. "You sure, sweetheart?" A brush of one fingertip across her nipple. "We should probably discuss—"

Haley yanked his mouth to hers and kissed him until they had to break apart for air. "Fuck discussions," she said and slipped her hand between them, pushing it into the front of his jeans and stroking the silken head of his cock that was peeking over the waistband of his underwear.

He groaned, hips thrusting forward.

She felt herself grow wetter, knew that she needed this man inside her or she would die.

Literally, it felt as though she would die if he didn't fuck her that second.

"Talk later," she panted, flicking the button of his jeans open, desperate to get both hands on him. "Fuck now."

His lips curved into a wicked grin. "That I can do." He yanked her T-shirt up and over her head, her bra followed a second later. He'd just cupped her breast and bent to take her nipple in his mouth when she heard a *crash*, then a shriek, then a "What the fuck?!"

FOURTEEN

Sam

WELL, this was awkward.

Maggie stood just inside the front door, a bowl of food overturned at her feet and fury in every line of her expression. She stepped over the pile of what looked to be noodles and strode toward them, eyes flashing.

Sam moved to stand in front of Haley, blocking her from view.

Her T-shirt had managed to hang itself on one of her barstools, so he snagged it then passed it to her.

"What in the fuck is going on?" Maggie snapped.

Sighing, Sam crossed his arms. "Maggie."

"Don't *Maggie* me—"

"This isn't what it looks like."

Sam's mouth clamped closed, and he spun around to face Haley. Um. What the hell was she talking about? *This* was exactly what it looked like. For fuck's sake, she'd been topless with her hand down his pants.

"Explain." Maggie.

"There's nothing to explain," he said. "This is between me and Haley."

Haley didn't look at him. "Mags. I'm sorry. I shouldn't have. I . . ."

Maggie, the woman he'd once thought would be his wife, didn't acknowledge Haley. Instead, she kept her brown eyes fixed on Sam. "How could you do this to my sister? You knew she had a crush on you." A shove to his chest. "What? Is this some sort of check mark on your bucket list, to sleep with sisters?"

"That's not fair—"

"You knew?" Haley shrieked, her cheeks going pink. "You knew, and you didn't say anything?"

Maggie shook her head, voice softening, the slightest note of pity lacing its way into her tone. "Oh kiddo, of course I knew. It was so obvious."

Sam had a lot of love for the girl who'd been his childhood sweetheart, but in that moment, he could have strangled her. It was a painful thing to witness, Haley wilting under her sister's tone and superior expression.

He tried to rescue the situation. "I didn't know. I swear, Haley. I mean I hardly noticed you until you came back into town, and I probably never would have even talked—"

Oh, fuck.

That wasn't rescuing. That was dive-bombing. Dropping a nuke on the situation and blowing it to fucking shreds.

Haley's face paled and hurt swam in her eyes.

"That's not what I meant—"

"Regardless," Maggie said, chiming in with perfectly terrible timing. "This is bad, Hays. You're vulnerable, and Sam isn't right for you."

"Vulnerable—" Haley began.

"Yes, you're hurt, and he's taking advantage."

Since that particular sentiment hit too close to home, it took a second for Sam to gather his wits.

"He absolutely isn't taking advantage," Haley said. "I mean, I know it was wrong to get involved with him—"

Wrong? Sam blinked. They were two adults and—

"*Of course*, he's taking advantage. Or rather, he's trying to assuage his guilt by being with—by making you feel good." She pointed at Sam. "This is what he does, Hays. He feels guilty and sticks around, and you have to be the one to stand strong and let him go."

"What the hell are you talking about?" Sam gritted out.

Maggie blinked, her face going carefully blank as she slipped out of her preaching attitude. It had always been hard to get her to shut up when she was going off on a tangent, but this absolutely took the cake. But finally, she did shut up, taking in what was no doubt a furious expression on his face because she bit her lip and flicked her gaze away.

Then Haley spoke, and his rage went to a whole new level.

"Look, I know he broke your heart and that you were really hurt and—"

Sam saw red. Literally, his skin went too tight, his teeth ground together so fiercely that he was surprised he didn't crack a fucking tooth, and a red haze tinted his vision.

Obviously, Maggie had never told Haley what had happened between them, what truly had ended their relationship. Sam had never said anything, never *would* have gone there because he was a fucking gentleman, but that Maggie had painted him like that to her sister . . .

His hands tightened into fists. Because fuck her.

Stand strong? Let him go? *Ha.* If anyone had broken hearts, it had been Maggie.

"Are we seriously going to go here?" he asked her.

Maggie paled, turned her gaze deliberately to Haley. "Maybe he's not taking advantage, but he's too—"

"Too what?" he asked, cold fury in those two syllables.

"I know what you mean," Haley said. Her eye flicked to the ground then back up to his. "You should go, Sam. This"—a cough—"let's face facts. This wasn't ever going to work out."

"What the hell are you talking about?" He reached for her, stopping when she cringed back. "We didn't even have a chance to—"

"Sam." She sighed. "You're *you* and I'm . . . *I'm* me. Let's face facts. We would have never gone anywhere anyway."

He frowned. "Haley, I'm not saying that I've fallen madly in love with you or that you're my soul mate or— We've just started getting to know each other again, but I like you—" He sucked in a breath. "I was hoping that we might—"

"What? Date? *Fuck?*" Haley let out an exasperated sigh. "Let's just leave it here, Sam. Let's just stop before someone gets hurt."

Yeah. Like him.

Again.

"That's the right decision," Maggie said.

Sam ignored her. "Is that what you want?"

Haley lifted her chin. "It's what I need, Sam. Brian broke me. I—I can't risk you doing to me what you did to Maggie."

"What did Brian—" Maggie began.

Sam had kept his eyes fixed on Haley's, looking for some sign of uncertainty or remorse.

He found neither.

Just perfect.

The Donovan sisters sure knew how to fuck with a guy's mind.

"Just go, Sam," Haley murmured.

He shook his head and strode for the door, stepping over the pile of noodles on the threshold. There, he paused and glared at Maggie. "I know we dated for six years, and both of us made plenty of mistakes during that time, but maybe you should share with your sister what actually happened between us." He pushed through the door. "Maybe then she wouldn't be using the past as an excuse to torpedo her future."

Silence before the door slammed behind him.

FIFTEEN

Haley

HALEY WATCHED Sam's SUV disappear down her driveway and couldn't stop the pang of remorse from coursing through her.

Had she just made the biggest mistake of her life, not hopping aboard the Sam train?

No. She'd jumped in headfirst once before, and look where that had gotten her.

"Well, good," Maggie said, brushing her hands down the front of her shirt. "That's a near miss." She bustled over to the spilled bowl and pasta, using her hands to scoop it up.

Yuck.

Carefully, Haley slid herself to the end of the counter and executed a perfect dismount onto her good leg. *Thank you, seven years of gymnastics.* From there, she maneuvered herself onto her scooter, grabbed a roll of paper towels and wheeled over to her sister.

"Here," she said. "I would offer to help—"

"But I wouldn't let you anyway," Maggie said, finishing their old joke.

As much as they ragged on their mom for never compromising, for always having to do it *her* way, Maggie was almost as bad. She was very particular and exacting and, frankly, that was exhausting sometimes.

But Haley had never really come up against it, or maybe she'd never pushed . . . same way as she dealt with her mom. It was easier to capitulate than fight over controlling every single detail, especially when she knew with one-hundred percent certainty that Maggie had her best interest in mind.

Except—

Except for the first time ever, Haley really wondered if Maggie really did have her best interest in mind. When it came to Sam, was her sister blind?

Was it old hurt? Protective sisterly love?

Or was there something else happening beneath the surface? Something that had happened between Maggie and Sam that Haley didn't understand.

"Mags?" she asked.

"What?"

"I—"

Her sister gathered up the bowl, dumping the contents in the trash and setting it into the sink.

"What—"

Maggie gathered up the dirty towels, rushing down the hall to throw them in the wash. When she came back into the room, she was carrying Haley's mop. "What a mess! I'd better get this cleaned up before you slip and break the other leg."

Her laughter was forced, and Haley debated what she should do. Obviously, Maggie didn't want to talk about what had gone down with her and Sam. She'd never been able to force her sister to do anything. *She* was the one to give in, to cave. Haley had absolutely zero skills in her social toolbox to help her deal with Maggie when she was like this. So, needless to say, she certainly couldn't force her sister to dish all. Not unless—

She dished first.

Fuck. She didn't want to talk about Brian, about her old job, about the myriad reasons she'd come home.

The past was the past, and they should leave it in the—

Ha. Now, *that* was a load of bull if she'd ever heard one. Haley had left the past in the past about as well as her mother let go of old grudges.

Which was not at all.

Could she talk about Brian? She'd already told some of it to Sam. Unwillingly to begin with, but she *had* felt better in the end.

Maybe this would just expand on that?

Maybe she could make herself *and* Maggie feel better.

Probably a pipe dream.

But it was worth a shot, right?

Right. She nodded and opened her mouth and just blurted, "Brian and I broke up."

Maggie froze in her mopping for a moment before resuming her left-right-front-back movement. Yes, her sister was particular enough about her day-to-day life that she even had a preferred technique for mopping.

Was it more pathetic that Haley knew her sister's chosen mopping pattern or that Maggie had a blueprint for everything, right down to the best way to soak up water from the floor, in the first place?

Either. Both.

She sighed, opened her mouth to expound.

"I surmised as much, considering you had your hand down Sam's pants when I first walked in." Maggie mopped faster. "I don't understand you, Haley. Are you desperate enough to take my seconds?"

Hurt sliced through her. "That's not fair."

"Or what?" Maggie was moving at warp speed now, the mop swooshing over the floor almost as quickly as her words shot like bullets into Haley's chest. "You never grew out of that pathetic crush. I mean, I swear it was so embarrassing to watch you mooning over him like a pitiful schoolgirl."

Tears stung Haley's eyes and she might have kicked her sister out of her house altogether, screamed and shouted and *hurt* her back, but this wasn't like Maggie at all.

Normally, her sister was nice, boarding on almost too nice.

She was particular but didn't lose her temper. Not ever. Hell, if someone didn't do tasks the way she preferred them, she was much more likely to thank the person before sneaking behind them to quietly redo it than yelling at them. Haley had rarely seen her sister raise her voice and she had never *ever* witnessed Maggie acting like this.

Mean. Horrible. Cruel.

Luckily, the shock of such a reversal in her sister's behavior meant that though Haley's feelings were hurt, she at least managed to hold on to a thin thread of rationality.

One that allowed her to say, "This isn't like you, Mags. Why are you acting like this?"

Maggie swallowed hard. "I'm not acting like anything. I'm trying to protect my sister is all." She lifted the mop and hurried back down the hall. Of course, her return to the kitchen was much slower.

Haley decided she'd had about enough. She positioned her scooter in front of the hall, blocking Maggie's path to escape.

Because she was smart enough to know that would probably be her sister's next move. Avoidance unless absolutely cornered. After which, she'd lash out and run. And the degree of lashing out she'd just experienced told Haley that the thing Maggie was hoping to avoid discussing was huge.

So, she blocked the hall and waited.

"Don't you want to know why Brian and I broke up?" she asked after her sister had stashed the mop and then turned back to the front of the house.

"Of course, I do," Maggie said, starting to inch around her. "I just—Tim texted and—"

Yeah. Nice try, Sis. Haley could see Maggie's phone sitting on the counter.

"Can you help me?" she asked, trying a different tack. "My leg's hurting, and I don't think I can get onto the couch."

Maggie sighed but stopped inching toward the front door and instead walked next to Haley as she wheeled herself to the sofa. "Do you need a pain pill?"

"No," Haley said. "Just a hand."

Maggie didn't argue, just slid a hand under Haley's arm and helped her transition, but when her sis would have pulled back, Haley grabbed her wrist.

"Mags." A plea. "Brian cheated on me. He—" She shook her head. "It was a good thing, ultimately, because I was in a bad place with him for a long time—"

"Did he hurt you?"

Finally, Haley saw a glimpse of her sister instead of the mean, avoidance monster.

"Not in the way you're thinking," she said. "But he was an asshole and managed to do a number on my confidence. For a long time, I thought . . . well, I *still* struggle with not measuring up, with not being smart or pretty enough to—" She broke off.

"To what?" Maggie asked.

"To—" Haley's eyes pricked. "I just—I know I can never measure up to you."

Maggie had been squatting next to her, knees floating above

the ground as she got settled, but at Haley's words, her sister's legs gave way, her knees hitting the carpet with a *thump*.

"If you knew—" A tear leaked from the corner of Maggie's eye. "If you knew what I did, then you'd understand that I'm the one who needs to live up to you, Hays. I—" She sniffed.

"I don't understand."

"I can't—" Maggie jumped to her feet. "I need to go."

"Mags—"

The sound of her front door slamming, for a second time that evening, echoed through her house.

SIXTEEN

Sam

SAM SIGHED as he plunked his ass into a booth in Henry's Place.

Named after a Darlington local, Henry, and started by Henry's dad, Brad, the diner was a Darlington staple with home-cooked food and killer recipes that had been in the Miller family for generations.

Not to say that Henry hadn't improved on the menu, because he most definitely had. He'd gone to culinary school and then had cooked under several famous chefs in New York City.

It was only after his dad had gotten sick that Henry came home.

He'd stayed when Brad passed on, cooking at the diner, tweaking a few much-loved menu items for the better, and watching out for his mom.

But for some reason, he'd never left.

Rumor had it that he'd left someone in New York, though

no one had ever been able to get the information out of Henry himself.

Sam picked up a menu and glanced at it, though he knew it by heart. It also helped that he usually ordered the same thing. Hamburger—medium—sweet potato fries, and water, because he liked to pretend to be a little healthy before he finished off his meal with a giant slice of Henry's chocolate cream pie.

Seriously the best.

Maybe he could become one of those people who medicated his feelings with food. He'd seen a study recently that said chocolate cured depression. He could totally do with an extra slice of pie.

He would also *totally* gain a spare tire.

Because he had a feeling that his emotions wouldn't be tempered in the least with chocolate or alcohol or—

"Your usual?" Tilly asked, coming over. A petite blonde in her early twenties, she often wore a smile that was as bright as her hazel eyes. She was also sweet, kind, and efficient.

"Yes. Thanks."

Sam often came in late after working, too exhausted to go home and cook, not when the diner was only a few blocks from his clinic.

Plus, it was a place with people. A place he could sit and listen and . . . feel like he belonged for a half a second.

Sigh.

He was being so fucking dramatic.

But Haley hadn't called or texted. She hadn't shown up and—

She couldn't show up anywhere, dickweed, he thought angrily. *Her ankle is broken.*

"Why the long face, Dr. Johnson?"

Sam's eyes flashed up at the same moment a stone dropped in his gut.

Esther.

AKA trouble.

"Hi, Esther. How's the kitten?"

She waved a hand. "Don't try to distract me by talking about Snuggles." But she pulled out her phone and extended it in his direction. "Adorable, as you can see." He barely had time to nod before she continued, "Anyway, I was just over there and saw you were by yourself. I thought Haley—*ah . . .*"

He'd made a rookie mistake.

He'd reacted.

And Esther was maybe more of an intensive investigator than Rob and all of the sheriff's office combined. Nothing slipped past her, especially nothing so obvious as a wince.

"Oh, so there is trouble in paradise?" She pulled up the note function on her phone. "Tell me all the details, I'll make it better."

"I didn't—"

Tilly set his plate down, took one look at Esther and her phone and all but ran off.

Traitor.

Esther tapped his hand. "How'd you screw up, Sam?"

He raised one brow. "So, it's *Sam* now?"

She smiled beatifically. "My little Sam, always so smart and trusting"—he snorted—"you know I can fix things for you. I love the idea of you and Haley together."

"Tell that to Haley," he muttered, shoving a fry into his mouth. "Or Maggie."

Esther stole the pickle from his plate. She knew all that happened in Darlington and that included the fact that he couldn't stand the bastardized version of cucumbers.

Either that or she really didn't give a shit and just did what she wanted.

Really, it could go either way.

"Well," she said, chomping on the pickle. "You did break Maggie's heart—"

That was enough. He shoved his plate away and stormed down the hall, stopping just shy of the bathroom to turn and drop his forehead against the wall. Esther would probably eat all his fries, and his burger would get cold just sitting there. Not that it mattered. The food, normally so filling and delicious, had tasted like sawdust.

So much for medicating with food.

He couldn't even do *that* right.

But Esther thought *he'd* been the one to end things with Maggie, that he'd been the bad guy, when in reality—

A cough.

Sam turned enough to see Henry himself standing behind him.

"Since you're not trying to dine and dash"—Henry jerked his head in the direction of an open door—"why don't you come into my office and not give Esther anything else to talk about?"

Sam glanced down the hall, saw Esther, fries sticking out of her mouth like sewing pins used to stick out of his mom's when she'd been working on a new quilting project. Esther's phone was pointed in his direction, probably cataloging his pathetic display for the whole town to see.

How had he once thought her social media channels entertaining?

Fine. It *was* supremely entertaining when he wasn't the sole focus.

He turned and followed Henry into his office.

"Hang tight," Henry said, after indicating the chair in front of his desk. He disappeared out of the door before Sam could respond then reappeared before he could really worry, two plates in his hands. "Chocolate, right?"

Sam nodded and accepted the plate as well as a fork Henry pulled from his apron pocket.

"So, you and Haley?" Henry asked around a bite of what looked to be lemon cream.

Sam sighed. "I'd thought—" He shook his head. "It wasn't to be."

"Like it wasn't to be with you and Maggie?"

"Fuck off." Sam dropped the plate on the desk and stood.

Henry was nonplussed and took another bite of his pie. "I'm guessing you didn't do the dumping, like all of Darlington assumes."

Sam had been on the threshold of the door when Henry spoke again and at the words, he froze, chin dropping to his chest.

"That's a no," Henry said. "So, why'd she dump you?"

He whirled around, glaring at Henry. "None of your business."

"Great," Henry replied, shoving another bite home, his next words slightly garbled. "I hate gossip. Shut up, sit down, and eat your pie."

Sam rolled his eyes, but he shut up, sat down, and started eating, glad when the pie started finally tasting like its usual deliciousness rather than cardboard.

"Haley's loyal to Maggie," Henry said when their slices were almost gone.

Sam grunted.

"She'd be hard-pressed to do anything that might hurt her sister."

"Yeah," he snapped. "Well, what about what Maggie *and* Haley did to hurt me?"

Henry set his fork down. "Now you sound like a pathetic whiner. Just talk to Haley, explain what happened. I'm sure once she understands—"

"I'm not going to spread all of Maggie's and my gossip over town." Sam set his own fork down. "We were finished years ago, anyway. It doesn't matter now."

A *plunk* as Henry dropped his boots onto his desk. "Except it obviously does."

Sam sighed. Because Henry was right. It *did* matter and—

"Why am I talking about this with you?"

The other man was several years younger than him and while they knew each other and were on friendly terms because of the diner and Sam's veterinary skills, it wasn't like they were besties hanging out every weekend.

Besties?

Now he was really losing it.

"You're discussing this with me because I'm infinitely wise and smart about all things with regards to the opposite sex."

"Yeah?" Sam grumbled. "If that's true, then why are you single?"

A shadow crossed Henry's face. "Let's just say that I'm infinitely wise at letting problems and miscommunications fester so much that they ruin a relationship from the inside out." He picked up both plates. "Don't let that be your fate, Sam. Not when you have a chance to work things out."

He left the office, but not before calling over his shoulder, "Food's on the house tonight. Word of advice, though, sneak out the back door before Esther loses patience and starts trying to find material for her next post."

Sam beat it out the back door, trying to ignore Henry's words.

He wasn't a glutton for punishment. He was done being hurt.

Sam was absolutely finished with the Donovan sisters.

SEVENTEEN

Haley

HALEY KNEW the knock at the door wouldn't be Sam, but her heart raced like it was anyway.

It had been a week since he'd left that night.

She missed him more than she'd thought possible.

But he hadn't returned the messages she'd left at the clinic checking up on him, hadn't stopped by . . . and it was probably for the best.

They—her with a man like *him*—would never have worked out anyway.

Plus, her brain was probably overestimating Sam's appeal, because she'd been cooped up with no one for company besides the occasional visit from her mom, sister, and Melissa, but even those were few and far between because the women close to her had their own lives which did not revolve around catering to her every whim.

Or extreme boredom.

Okay, so there was that too.

The knock came again, and Haley called, "Coming!" as she wheeled her way to the front door.

The knob hadn't rattled, a sure sign of her mother on the other side trying to let herself in, so Haley hurried over, eager to see who was visiting.

She wasn't prepared to unlock the door and see her sister's tear-streaked face.

"Mags," she said. "What's—"

"Have you seen *this?*" her sister shrieked, shoving her phone into Haley's line of sight.

"Uh . . ." She tried to read the headline in . . . apparently there was a Facebook group for Darlington? It was called— rather unoriginally, she thought, Darlington Drama. "What—?" She snatched the phone from Maggie's grip, saw its adminis- trator was Esther.

Of course, it was Esther.

Lord of the Banana Cream Pies, please give her strength.

Because the lead story was, Haley Bear Breaks Hearts Home and Abroad, the tale of her broken engagement and "Our Own Dr. Johnson's Freshly Broken Heart."

Thankfully, Esther didn't really have any details about her broken engagement with Brian, but she did have a picture of Sam looking . . . well, heartbroken.

Maggie stormed by her, opening the cabinet door beneath the sink and pulling out some cleaning supplies. In seconds she was scrubbing the crap out of Haley's kitchen counter.

Sighing, Haley shut and locked the door then turned back to her sister. "I'm sure it's—"

"Don't say it's not nothing!" Maggie wailed.

Haley rolled her eyes, called on the Lord of Banana Cream again—at least the terrible innuendo tempered her irritation— and wheeled herself to the kitchen. "Mags," she ordered, grabbing her sister's wrist and all but wrestling the squirt bottle out of her hand. "*Stop.*"

Maggie froze, chest heaving.

"What the *hell* is going on?"

Her sister hung her head. "You're going to hate me."

"I couldn't hate you." Haley bumped her shoulder. "Then I'd have to like mom and we both know I can't do that."

Maggie snorted, but tears leaked out of the corners of her eyes. "I was horrible," she said. "I deserve to be hated." A shaking exhale. "I deserve for Sam to hate *me.*"

Haley's heart skipped a beat. "What happened, Mags?"

Her sister sucked in another breath then released it. "It was my fault. All of it. I just—" She wiped her face. "I respected what you were doing. *So much.* I hope you know that. Moving to California, going after your dream, doing something you loved, and damn all the consequences." She blew out a breath. "I couldn't even leave Salt Lake. Sam wanted me to go, but I couldn't—"

"Why?"

She sniffed. "Because I'd found someone else."

"You—" Haley sat up. "*What?*"

"I was young and stupid and so mad that Sam wasn't around." She shook her head. "He was studying and working, for God's sake, and I—"

"You cheated on him."

Maggie nodded.

Haley sucked in a breath. *Shit.* She'd . . . well, she'd really, *seriously* fucked up. Sam was—

Damn. Her chin dropped to her chest.

She needed to apologize, needed to hobble her ass down the street on her crutches and beg for Sam's forgiveness. She'd put all the blame for the breakup on his shoulders and he'd been the one wronged. But . . . right at that moment, her sister needed Haley to listen more than Sam needed his apology.

"I didn't tell him," Maggie said softly. "I just got swept away with the whole thing, and I didn't tell Sam that things weren't working out. He was studying and picking up extra shifts so we could live together in Minnesota, and I was"—her voice cracked —"I was hiding my engagement ring so that I could fuck around with Bradley."

Haley couldn't lie that she was relieved to hear that Tim wasn't the man Maggie had cheated on Sam with.

That would have made Sunday dinners awkward.

"So, what happened?" she asked, guiding them back into the living room. She sank onto one half of the couch.

Maggie stayed standing but her eyes slid closed. "Affairs have a shelf life. Someone slips up or gets tired of—" She pressed her lips together. "Bradley found out I was engaged and told Sam."

Haley touched Maggie's cheek. "And you lost both of them."

A nod. "Yeah." A long slow exhale and she opened her eyes, regret swimming in the coffee depths. "Rightfully so, of course."

"That's why you were so devastated when you moved home," Haley said. "Why didn't you tell me?"

"It's the worst thing I've ever done in my life," she said. "I didn't want you to think I was a horrible person, even if I was." Maggie sighed. "It was easier in a lot of ways to just let Sam take the fall, especially since he was hundreds of miles away." She sat next to Haley on the couch. "But enough about me and my screwed-up ways, why didn't you tell me about Brian? I'm assuming the cheating isn't a new development."

"No," Haley murmured. "It wasn't. But it *is* a big part of the reason I needed to come home. The memories in California were just too painful." She shook her head. "No. That's not completely it either. Yes, it *was* painful, but I also didn't want to admit I failed, I guess. Your life seemed so perfect that I guess I needed to compete somehow." She tugged Maggie's wrist, pulling her in for a hug. "I'm sorry I assumed that you were always infallible, it wasn't exactly fair to shove you into a box like that."

Maggie sniffed. "I liked being infallible."

"You like things carefully arranged and black and white." Haley chuckled. "We all make mistakes, Mags. We all mess up sometimes."

"It wasn't just a mistake." Her sister's chest shuddered. "I—"

"Hush." Haley gripped Maggie by the shoulders and shook her gently. "It was a shitty thing to do, we both know that." A nod. "But I still am so sorry it happened. To both of you."

She *was* sorry. That Maggie had been so miserable, she'd done something incredibly hurtful to the person she'd loved. That she'd been young and stupid and immature.

That she hadn't felt like she could talk to Haley about it.

And also she began to wonder if perhaps Brian's reasons for cheating had been less about her and more about whatever had been going on in his own messed-up mind.

Maybe he'd been miserable and hadn't been able to—

Or maybe he was just an asshole.

Either. Both. Because while Sam might be mature enough to forgive Maggie, Haley thought that forgiving her ex and former friend were going to take a bit longer.

Work in progress, remember?

Her sister's laugh was brittle as she pulled back. "*I'm* sorry I was such an idiot that I let one of the best men I've ever known go. That I wounded him so deeply he's still alone. That he somehow managed to forgive me when I can't seem to forgive myself."

"Do you—" Haley cut herself off, uncertain she had the right to ask the question bouncing around her brain.

"No, ask," Maggie said. "We've spent far too much of our lives not asking the hard questions, leaving things alone because we didn't want to rock the boat." She dropped her head to Haley's shoulder. "I love you. So much. And, God, I'm so sorry I said those things. I didn't mean them . . . I just—"

"Wanted to be an ostrich for a little while longer?"

She shuddered. "You know how I feel about ostriches."

Haley did. Which was the reason she'd brought it up. Her sis had an unreasonable fear of the large, flightless bird. Probably because Haley had watched a ton of nature documentaries as a kid and both of them had nightmares about the one that had included a scene of an ostrich disemboweling a hyena that had been trying to steal its egg.

"You know what I really want to understand?" Haley asked.

Maggie flinched but raised her chin. "What do you want to know?"

"Why in the hell didn't our parents monitor our TV time?"

Maggie snorted and then they were laughing or crying, or maybe both. Either way, it was long minutes before they got it together.

"I'm so, so sorry, Hays. I don't know how you or Sam could possibly forgive me." She covered her face with her hands. "You guys should date, keep exploring things"—a sniff—"Great. Now I sound like I'm trying to play the martyr, but seriously, I think you'd be great for each other, and just because I let all of my regret from the past bubble up and—" Her shoulders dropped. "I hurt you and I hurt Sam. Again. I'm seriously the worst."

Haley lightly punched her arm. "Honestly, it's kind of refreshing to see that you're not perfect."

Maggie made an outraged noise.

"It's a breath of fresh air to see that you're a normal human being that makes mistakes. *Ow.*" Her sister swatted her back, but harder. "See? You even beat up innocent injured women."

"You're the worst," Maggie muttered.

"I love you." Haley rested her head on her sister's shoulder.

"I love you, too." A bump of Haley's head. "Now, ask your question from before."

"It's a doozy," Haley warned.

Maggie straightened, mimed putting on armor. "I'm ready."

A deep, bolstering breath. "I was going to ask if you wish that you hadn't cheated . . . that you were still with Sam."

Maggie stilled for a long moment, considering.

"No," she finally said. "It led me to Tim, and the life I have with him is more than I could have ever imagined." A pause. "But I do regret that I hurt Sam. It's like this huge cauldron of shame that never fully goes away. I did something horribly wrong, and it's probably a fitting punishment that I'm not sure I'll be able to get over it."

Equal parts of relief and empathy filled Haley.

Because . . . while this conversation had made her see that she obviously owed Sam a giant apology, she also knew she'd been using that trademark Donovan avoidance with him even before she'd hurt him.

Yes, she'd kissed him. Yes, she thought to hop on the ride for however long he would accept her. But at no point had she considered that Sam might well and truly like her, that he might see her as a desirable woman he wanted to date. She'd just assumed—

No. She'd *distanced* herself because that kept her heart safe.

She deserved better. They *both* deserved better.

He should be in a relationship with someone who thought he deserved all the happiness the world, who was willing to be open and to put themselves out there. Who was firmly *in* with both of her feet.

Broken ankle aside, she hadn't been in.

But revelations aside, Maggie was still waiting for a response, and Haley knew they'd shared about as much emotion as they could stand. So, she lightened her tone and said, "Shit, Sis, you need help."

A snort followed by a side hug. "Now, that's probably the most truthful thing you've said all day."

"Great." Haley picked up the TV remote. "I'm brilliant and truthful *and* funny—"

"I didn't say *that*," Maggie teased.

"Ignoring you," Haley sang. "I'm brilliant because I'm ordering us a pizza and you're going to call Tim and say you need some sister time so we can binge our night away on nature documentaries."

Maggie smiled. "Make it the new season of *Queer Eye* and I'm in."

Haley pretended to consider that and Mags smacked her. "Abuse," she said. "Jeez! Okay, fine, grab the ice cream from the freezer so we can have dessert first, and you're on."

***

"Go," Haley mouthed, waving her sister off the following evening, after having staked out Sam's house with binoculars.

Yes, binoculars.

But it turned out she could see Sam's driveway from her living room window by watching from just the right angle and using . . . binoculars.

Stalker one-oh-one, sign her up.

But Haley's use of the magnifying device aside, she'd been able to see Sam drive up and settle in for the evening. She'd called Maggie and begged her for a ride several driveways down, since she didn't trust herself to make it that far on crutches and her scooter would only be bogged down in the gravel.

After another of Haley's shooing gestures, Maggie finally lifted her hand in resignation and reversed out of the driveway.

Like her own, this one was gravel.

So, the car and even her crutches made a lot of noise.

And the fact that the door remained shut did not speak well of her plan.

She might be crutching the distance between Sam's house and her own anyway.

Up the couple of steps to Sam's porch, a moment of balancing before she was able to ring the doorbell.

No response.

Haley bit her lip. Rang again.

Still nothing.

"Shit," she muttered, trying to convince herself he just hadn't heard, that maybe his bell was broken. So, she carefully shifted her weight and knocked on the door.

No answer.

Okay, so clearly this had been a stupid idea.

She turned, started to make her way down the steps. Sam wouldn't talk to her, wouldn't forgive her. And why should he? She'd made assumptions without letting him explain his side. She'd thrown away the new, fragile thing they'd just started building.

This was her own doing.

"Dammit." She took one hand off a crutch to wipe her face–sweat, not tears . . . which was a lie, but she only had so much dignity left, okay?

The door swung open and she whirled around then immediately lost her balance.

"*Ah!*"

Sam caught her.

Before she came close to colliding with the steps or the gravel or even the rough planks of the porch, he caught her.

Dammit, *why* had he caught her?

She deserved—

He cradled her against his chest, eyes studying her closely, but just when his expression seemed to soften, Sam's face turned to granite.

His hands were gentle though.

He deposited her carefully onto the steps, propped her crutches so they were next to her.

"Stay," he growled.

And it was then she noticed that he was only wearing a towel and his hair was wet.

So he hadn't been avoiding her.

He'd been in the shower.

Genius observation. But it wasn't entirely her fault that her brain was malfunctioning, not when there was so much tan skin and so many hard muscles on display. His chest glistened and that towel was . . . so *precarious*. Her fingers itched to knock it askew, to encourage it to drop to the porch, but one look at his face stalled the notion.

"Stay," he repeated and waited for her to nod. But when she opened her mouth to apologize, he turned and swept into the house, shutting the door firmly behind him.

She was getting *really* tired of doors being slammed in her face.

Haley had just stood up, ready to barge into the house and demand he hear her apology, when the door whipped open again. Sadly for her, he'd gotten dressed.

He took one look at Haley on her feet and sighed before sweeping by her and unlocking the doors of his SUV with a *beep*. A tug of the handle to open the passenger's side before he was heading back in her direction.

"Sam—"

He lifted her up into his arms again, swiftly deposited her into the passenger's seat. "Buckle in."

"I'm—"

A sigh as he reached over to secure her seat belt.

"Sor—"

The door slammed.

Again.

For the love of—

He yanked open the driver's door and dropped himself into the seat. "Sam—" He turned the key. "I'm really—" Blared the music. "Sorry—" Revved the engine as he reversed.

Haley sighed and switched off the radio.

He switched it back on.

Good gravy, how childish was he going to be?

She pressed the dial, turned it back off.

Less than her, apparently, because he left the music off.

"I'm sorry," she said into the silence.

Sam's only response was to maneuver into her driveway, turn off the engine, and then shove his way out of his side of the car. He came around and swung her up into his arms.

She cupped his cheek. "Maggie told me."

He shuddered and deposited her on her porch steps before returning back for her purse and crutches.

"I shouldn't have—"

He dug into her purse, extracted her keys to unlock her front door. "I can't do this."

"What?"

He scooped her up again, carrying her inside as she stared at him dumbly. *That was it?* He was just going to give up at the first sign of trouble? Except wasn't that what she'd done.

But she was trying to *undo* it. Trying to give them a chance at something that might mean everything.

"We need to talk—"

Sam deposited her on the couch, wheeled her scooter over to her, and plunked her purse on the table, setting her keys next to it. Her crutches went by the door, which he started to close behind himself.

"*Sam.*"

His only response was a shake of his head.

This time when the door shut, it didn't slam.

But it hurt all the same.

"No," she said. She wasn't going to let him do this, let him throw their chance at something good and meaningful all away because she'd been an idiot. Haley grabbed her purse from the table, rummaging around inside until she found her cell. It only took her a few seconds to dial a number she knew by heart.

"I need help," she said when the call was picked up.

EIGHTEEN

Sam

SATURDAY MORNING BROUGHT with it more clouds, rain, and biting wind. Sam had planned on being in the clinic all day, and so he hadn't bothered with more than a cursory check of the weather.

But best-laid plans and all that.

He'd gotten the call just after five in the morning from Hank, a local cattle rancher. Hank had been out on his normal A.M. rounds and had discovered a calf stuck in the mud and near-death. Pouring rain had made the conditions even worse.

By the time Sam had made it to the ranch, Hank had pulled the calf free, wrapped it in a blanket, and met him at the barn. They'd gone inside, trying to keep the calf warm as he'd worked on the young animal.

Ultimately, it hadn't mattered because Sam had been forced to euthanize the calf.

Hank had cried, Sam had felt like shit, and Saturday had continued on in Friday's fucked up track. He'd rushed back to his house for a shower in rain-soaked clothes for the second time in a week, wind and water seeping through the damaged driver's side door, and had been ten minutes late for his first appointment.

Saturdays were busy and on that particular day they were absolutely slammed, so it was just perfect that Michelle had needed to leave midway through the morning.

Not her fault, he knew, that she'd spiked a fever. Anyone looking at her could tell she was feeling miserable, and he couldn't exactly have one of his employees being patient zero of the town's latest flu epidemic.

So, he'd put his head down and slogged through the long list of appointments.

He'd barely even had time to miss Haley.

Haley.

Aw shit.

He didn't want to think about Haley or Maggie or the fact that he'd been burned twice in his life by the Donovan sisters. He needed to finish his final two appointments of the day and then go home and crack open a beer.

Or ten.

Jane knocked on the back door and popped her head into the hallway that spanned the space behind the patient rooms. "We've had a call from Melissa Cooper. Rocco's gotten into something and cut his paw. She thinks he might need stitches. Should I refer her over to the emergency clinic?"

Sam sighed. "No, tell her to bring him in."

He wasn't going to send his friend on a three-hour drive for something he could handle in half that.

Jane nodded and closed the door. He picked up the chart for his next patient—a ten-year-old and very temperamental Maltipoo named Precious—and girded his loins. Two—no, three —more patients, and then he'd been done with this horrible day.

Thankfully, Precious took pity on him that day, and the exam, shots, and nail trim went relatively easily, and the bearded dragon he saw for his last official appointment of the day was a fun and interesting case.

Turned out the little guy wasn't a fan of calcium worms and needed crickets added to his diet.

A quick trip to the coffee pot for a shot of caffeine before he gathered suture supplies and pushed through the door of exam room three. Immediately, he realized Jane had duped him and vowed to pay her back with multiple boxes of filing at his earliest opportunity, because seriously, the last thing he wanted to be dealing with at the end of his long and shitty day was this.

Haley.

With regret in her gaze and an apology on her lips.

He whirled and pushed back out the door, walking down the hall and shoving the supplies back into their proper spots as he went. He needed to get the fuck out of here, get his head on straight so that—

"Sam." Haley followed him, the wheels of her scooter squeaking against the industrial tiles. "I need to apol—"

"No apology needed," he said, dropping the last of the supplies into a drawer.

He kept walking, moving to his computer at the end of the counter and closing out what he absolutely had to. The rest of it could wait until Monday.

A touch on his arm. "Sam."

He moved away. "It's fine. I get it—"

"So, Maggie cheated," she said, all conversational-like.

Fuck. She'd said her sister had told her. But he'd hoped . . .

What?

That she'd never discovered how pathetic he was?

Shit.

"And you know it's not your fault, right?"

He shrugged, turning to meet Haley's eyes. And there was pity in her gaze. Awesome, so Maggie had definitely confessed all. He'd basically pressed her to, but Haley looking at him like that, like he was some poor wounded creature . . . well, it really didn't feel great.

Fine. Because frankly, it felt like shit and the perfect addendum to his day.

"Sam?"

He grunted, shrugged off his lab coat and hung it on the proper hook.

More squeaking wheels, but even if Haley hadn't had the equivalent of a cat's bell on its collar in her scooter, he still would have known when she moved closer. Her scent—roses—drifted forward, inundating his senses, and his nape prickled, instinctively knowing that she was only inches away.

This time he couldn't force himself away from her touch, not when she wrapped her arms around him and pressed her breasts against his spine.

Fuck. He wanted her so badly.

"I'm just saying that I know it takes time to accept it as truth, but what Maggie did was on her. Not you. Not in any way. As for us"—she sucked in a breath—"I was scared. I seized an opportunity to run because I'm fucked up and I was feeling unworthy and unlovable, and I like you. A lot." She squeezed him tighter. "I'm still recovering in the confidence department because I couldn't imagine how you might possibly be able to like *me*."

He dropped his chin to his chest.

Haley didn't say anything further, just held him, and the anger he'd been stoking for close to a week disappeared.

"Dammit, sweetheart," he finally muttered and carefully disentangled himself so he could turn around and see her. "I like you. A whole hell of a lot, but I can't keep doing this." Her face fell, and he cupped her cheek. "I can't keep reassuring you that I like you, that I want to get to know you better. I want to take you out, see if the chemistry we have can develop into something more, but . . ."

"But what?"

"I need you to be all in, too," he said. "I need you not to have one foot out the door, expecting me to leave, to all of a sudden turn on you like that asshole did."

Her lips parted and she sucked in a breath. "I—"

"You deserve better for yourself, sweetheart. You're fun and kind and incredibly smart, not to mention beautiful"—she shook her head and he shook his in response—"That, right there. You don't see yourself clearly."

"I'm not—"

He rested his hand just above her heart. "You are the most beautiful woman I've ever seen. Not just the outside"—he tapped lightly—"but here, too. You're generous and sweet and—"

Her lips twitched. "Now I feel like I'm fishing for compliments."

Sam cupped her cheek. "No need for fishing. You deserve all those."

"And more?"

He chuckled and pressed a kiss to her forehead. "See? Funny *and* sweet. You deserve everything you want, baby."

"And what if what I want is you?"

"Then I'm yours."

NINETEEN

Haley

SAM DROVE Haley home in silence, but it wasn't like the taut quiet from her days with Brian. This was comfortable, neither of them needing to fill the air with words, their hands laced and resting on his thigh.

It was the biggest leap she'd ever taken, moving to California aside, and certainly the biggest gamble she'd taken with the opposite sex.

Haley had put herself out there, and Sam . . . well, he'd accepted her.

But he'd demanded that she be all in, too.

Could she possibly—?

Fuck yes, she could. For Sam, for a chance at something that meant more than any of her past relationships, she could not be scared for once. She could dive in and learn every little idiosyncrasy that made Sam . . . Sam. And she could damn well let him in enough to understand all the strange pieces that made her Haley Donovan.

It was funny, because even yesterday she would have said she'd given Brian *everything*, but the past week had taught her that was a lie.

She was really good at distance and it had existed even when she'd been at her most vulnerable with Brian.

She'd always held part of herself back. Always.

And he'd known.

Yes, he was an asshole, a terrible person who'd preyed on all her insecurities, who'd wounded her deeply by betraying her, but, truthfully, Haley had never been all in with the relationship.

Hence, her being less upset about losing him and more upset over the fact that she couldn't keep a man but Maggie could—

God. She was seriously screwed up.

"What just went through your mind?" Sam asked.

And so, Test One of their dating relationship was upon them. Did she prevaricate, avoid the issue? Or did she—

Haley told the truth.

Sam listened patiently as she worked it out—basically verbally vomiting all the thoughts swirling around her brain. When she was done, he squeezed her hand and lifted it to his mouth, pressing a soft kiss to the back of it.

"Thank you," he said. "I think that was the part that hurt me the most with Maggie. I shouldered all of this responsibility, thought it was my fault that she'd jumped into bed with someone else when ultimately, it wasn't really about me at all."

"Right." She leaned her head on his shoulder. "She was the one who was missing something. Same as Brian. And no matter how hard we tried, that *something* they were missing wasn't going to be able to come from me. Or you."

Sam nodded, kissed the top of her head. "Insightful."

She turned so her lips could smack against his shoulder. "Way too patient."

The half of his mouth that she could see curved up.

Haley felt her own lips curl into a smile. Her heart was buoyant, anticipation and hope in her blood. This—Sam—was the start of something really, *really* good.

She just knew it.

———

"COME ON, HOP-A-LONG," Sam teased her as she crutched her way to his SUV the next evening.

He'd driven her home the previous night, depositing her onto her porch with a, "Go to dinner with me tomorrow?"

As if she could say no to that.

But she had demanded one thing before she'd agreed.

"Only if you give me your number."

He'd tilted his head, tapped a finger to his chin. "Hmm. I'm not sure—"

"Sam!"

He'd tugged her into his arms and stolen a laughing kiss, and pretty soon she was laughing, too, especially when they broke apart and he held up a hand with a magician-like flourish, her cell resting in his palm.

A few taps later, and he'd input his number.

"M'lady," he quipped, presenting it to her with another flourish, albeit a knightly one this time.

She'd taken it, carefully stashed it into her pocket. "You're a dork."

He'd bowed, pressed another smiling kiss to her mouth. "I'll double check my appointments tomorrow, but seven maybe?"

She'd nodded, and he'd clumped down the steps, yanked open his SUV's dented driver's side door but not getting in until she'd pushed through her own door and had shut it. Only then did he buckle up and drive away.

Haley knew. She'd watched.

It had been pretty much her best front door goodbye ever . . . okay, it was her best good night, no qualifier, just her and Sam being dorks, giggling and smiling and—

A hand cupped her cheek. "Are you feeling okay?" Sam asked. "We don't have to go anywhere, I can cook—"

This man.

She placed her hand over his, and because she was on crutches and he was so much taller than her and she only had one good foot to stand on tiptoe, she said, "Get down here and kiss me."

Sam didn't hesitate, just bent and slanted his mouth across hers. And as things seemed to happen with this particular man, their kiss quickly escalated from sweet and soft to scorching and intense. Her crutches fell to the ground, but Sam had her, hitching his arm around her waist and lifting her so she was sitting on the hood of the SUV and he was standing between her spread thighs.

Now *that* was something she could get behind.

"You're so fucking beautiful," he said.

"I—"

He kissed her again, slipping his tongue into her mouth to tangle with hers, angling her head so their mouths fit together just right. It was . . . fucking incredible.

So much so that when they finally pulled back gasping for air—or rather when she ripped her lips away, puffing like a locomotive while Sam trailed his mouth along the line of her jaw to nip at her earlobe then kissed the spot just beneath it that never failed to make her shiver—she said, "Maybe we should forget dinner and—"

A wicked smile curved Sam's lips and he kissed her again, scooped her into his arms.

Thank God, because if the man didn't get inside her in the next five seconds, she was—

Going to find herself in the passenger seat of Sam's SUV.

"Uh—"

Another press of his lips. A *click* as he snapped her seat belt in place. Then his lips were on hers again, moving in a rhythm that had her arching up against him, desperate now to have him close.

This time he pulled back with a curse. "You're dangerous to my health, woman." A glare, but a teasing one that quickly became laced with tenderness, his hazel eyes warming. "I like you, sweetheart. A lot. And I think you kinda, sorta like me"— she snorted—"so, let's do this right."

TWENTY

Sam

SAM HELD the door open to the diner as Haley wheeled herself through. He'd stashed her scooter in the back of his car because he knew just crutching down her gravel driveway was already tough enough. She might as well use the scooter whenever the opportunity presented itself.

The diner was busy, a half-dozen groups waiting in the lobby for tables. But such was Saturday night in Darlington. Henry's Place was the place to go for the best food in town and also hub central for town gossip.

So, him bringing Haley to the diner was sending a message to every person in Darlington.

She was important to him. They were serious.

Yes, it was too early for that particular train of thought, but he was having it anyway.

He wanted Haley and not just to see how things went or to investigate the possibility of what might be. She was . . . home.

Or at least, Sam never felt more himself than when he was with her.

Hence, dinner at Henry's Place.

Sam waved at the hostess, Kara, who in turn lifted both hands to indicate they'd be waiting about ten minutes. He shot her a thumbs up then turned back to Haley.

"Stitches still coming out tomorrow?" He gently untangled a strand of her ponytail that had tucked itself under the bandage on her forehead.

She smiled up at him. "You tired of the Frankenstein look?"

A gentle kiss to the corner of the bandage. "You make stitches hot."

"Bitches got stitches?" She snorted. "Is that the new fashion trend?"

"I must have missed that in my latest issue of *Cosmopolitan*."

Haley wheeled herself a little closer, her breasts brushing against his chest. Sam bent, eyes on her mouth, suddenly wishing they were back in her driveway and he hadn't insisted on this date.

Why had he insisted on this date?

She licked her lips.

He leaned down and—

Click.

Sam blinked, glanced away from the dangerous distraction that was Haley, and saw that Esther had her phone pointed in their direction.

"Dammit," she muttered. "I could have sworn I'd turned that camera sound off." Her eyes shot to his, and she held up a very expensive, top of the line cell. "New phone," she said, flashing him a smile that was less chagrined and more satisfied.

"Esther!" Haley said, glancing between the older woman and Sam. "You were *not* taking pictures of us."

"Haley, girl," Esther said. "I'm glad to see you and Sam worked things out. How are you feeling?"

Haley crossed her arms. "Nice try, missy. That had better not be going on your Facebook page," Haley said.

"Of course not." Sam's shoulders relaxed. "It's going on my Instagram. Facebook is for old people." His eyes met Haley's, the obvious comment on the tip of his tongue. Esther *was* old, almost ancient.

She shook her head, lifted her lips to his ear. "She may be a million years old, but she's also way cooler than us."

"I heard that!" Esther said. "I—"

"Can't hear me saying that in your hurry to document these two, you forgot your to-go box?" Henry walked into the waiting area and handed Esther a container. "No?" he said, mouth twitching when she didn't respond. "Hmm. Funny how that works."

Esther narrowed her eyes. "Just because you make a good sandwich doesn't mean that you can be smart with me, young man."

"I love you, too, Esther," Henry said, kissing her cheek and pointing to an unoccupied table for two in the corner of the diner. "Kelly's booth"—Kel and Henry had been best friends since grade school and one of the perks of that was a permanent table with her name on it in the restaurant—"is open, jump on in there."

Sam thanked him and indicated for Haley to go ahead of him, but before they could move too far they heard Esther ask, "Are *you* dating anyone right now, Henry?"

Henry choked.

Haley snorted.

Sam grinned.

Because they all knew what was coming next.

"I know just the perfect girl . . ."

"Run," Haley whispered out of the corner of her mouth. "Before Esther turns her evil genius attention back to us."

Sam mimed a heroic push of Haley's scooter. "Save yourself!" he hissed and followed her as she giggled her way to the table.

"Henry's going to kill us," she said once they'd sat down.

Sam glanced over his shoulder, saw that Henry was still cornered by Esther, who was now showing him something on her phone. Probably pictures of that perfect girl she had for him.

"Meh," he said, shrugging. "It's about time he had a turn. Henry needs a girl."

"Or a guy," Haley added.

"Or a guy," Sam agreed. "And we both know that Esther will find him that right person."

"Agreed." She unfolded her napkin, plunked it into her lap. "If I didn't know better, I'd think she'd coerced those deer into jumping in front of our cars." A pause. "Oh! I've been meaning to ask you, what about *your* car? When are you going to get that door fixed?"

The waitress, Tilly, came over with glasses of water, setting them on the table in front of them. "I'll be back in just a second to get your orders," she said and hurried off to another booth.

He winced when Haley looked at him expectantly.

She wouldn't like what he was about to tell her, and she'd definitely feel guilty about it.

"I'm actually thinking about dealing with it. I'm due for a new car anyway."

"What?" she asked. "Your SUV is practically brand new."

It was. He'd splurged for a new one, complete with heated seats and remote start because those early mornings driving out to the ranches were cold as fuck and because he worked hard for his money, dammit, so he could have one nice, frivolous thing.

A shrug.

"Sam—"

Tilly popped back over, and they spent the next few minutes ordering food. Once she'd gone again, Haley fixed him with a look. "Spill."

"Don't feel bad," he began, "because I believe we've already established that I was the one at fault—"

"Oh Lord. Do *not* tell me that my inept blasting of Backstreet Boys totaled your car."

"Okay," he said. "I won't tell you that." He took a sip of water.

"Sam!"

"It was the deer's fault, remember?"

Haley wrinkled her nose. "Oh my God. I—shit. I'm *so* sorry—"

She was so fucking gorgeous and sweet and . . . he really wanted to kiss her.

So, he did.

He leaned right across the table and cut off her stammering with his lips. It was only supposed to be a moment of brief contact, a brush of two mouths, but then Haley wrapped a hand around his nape and pulled him back down.

The diner faded, the other patrons, the table's edge that was digging into his stomach disappeared.

It was just him and Haley and—

A *whoop* made them both jump.

Cheeks flushing, she retreated, groaning and putting her hands over her face. "I didn't mean to—"

"Get it, girl!"

Esther.

They both looked at each other and shook their heads.

But they were smiling.

And before they'd eaten their meal, all of Darlington knew

that Sam Johnson and Haley Donovan were back to being an item.

Small town life at its finest.

TWENTY-ONE

Haley

"So, do you think that purple or pink goes best with my cast?" Haley asked Melissa.

"You can't wear a T-shirt on a date," Melissa said.

"Why not?"

Slender arms crossed. "Do you or do you not want to sleep with this man as soon as possible?"

"Uh, that's a definite yes."

"Good," Melissa said. "Then no T-shirts." She began to rifle through Haley's closet.

"Sam *likes* my T-shirts," Haley argued.

"Yes. I'm sure he likes whatever you wear. The man is absolutely crazy about you." Melissa pulled out a dress, considered it, then tucked it back away. "The point is that you've got a stubborn man who's trying to be honorable, and he thinks that means giving you more time to get used to the idea of you two dating."

"I don't want more time," Haley muttered.

Melissa pointed her finger toward the ceiling. "Exactly."

Haley wasn't exactly sure what that *exactly* meant, but her friend had thrown her a bone in the best possible way by bringing her both food and a break from the boredom that was surrounding her.

Three weeks since the accident.

One more before the hospital would allow her back for desk duty.

Three more till the fucking cast came off.

Ugh.

Okay, so maybe that ugh was less from missing work and more from missing Sam.

She'd only seen him three times in the last week. Once during their date the previous Sunday—after which he'd dropped her on her porch with a scorching kiss that had fueled more than satisfied—then briefly on Monday when they'd devoured the pizza he'd brought them for dinner before he'd been called to an emergency at the clinic. Tuesday, Wednesday, and Thursday, he'd been a few towns over, assisting a neighboring vet with vaccinations and deworming for cattle on a slew of ranches. Friday and Saturday, the other vet had returned the favor for the Darlington ranches.

He'd come by the previous evening, but after a single glance, Haley had sent him home.

Exhaustion had pulled at the contours of his face, his skin was pale and waxy, and the dark circles under his eyes were no joke.

So, home to sleep.

And she'd spent another evening on the couch entertaining herself.

Which sounded dirty, but unfortunately for her wasn't. On a side note, and why she'd begged for Melissa's expertise that evening, was that Haley was definitely ready for dirty.

Desperate for it really.

Sam had texted earlier, asking her to dinner again—not that she'd ever tell the man no. She loved spending time with him and also she had a plan.

And that plan did *not* involve Henry's Place on a busy Sunday night.

That plan involved getting *busy* on a Sunday night.

Wow.

She shook her head at herself.

Clearly, she'd been alone too much because those puns were *bad*.

"What are you grinning about? Wait, I don't think I want to know. What about this?" Melissa held up a black dress from the back of Haley's closet.

Haley could have kissed her. "*That's* perfect! Miss, you're awesome."

"Yeah, *that* I know," Melissa said and searched through the huge duffle bag she'd brought with her. In no time at all, she had Haley stylized to perfection. "Your feet are bigger than mine. But these"—she pulled out a pair of clunky heels from the closet—"will work perfectly. Or the left one will anyway," she teased.

"Hilarious," Haley said, but she hugged Melissa anyway. "Thank you."

"Aw, young love," Melissa crooned.

"Ha. As if you and Rob have room to talk," she accused. "The two of you are so lovely-dovey it's almost puke-worthy."

Melissa sat down on the edge of the bed. "That took a lot of work, Haley Bear."

She lifted her brows. "Really?"

"It's a cute nickname."

"It's—" Haley shrugged. "Okay, it could be worse. But . . . things really are okay with you and Rob, right?"

Melissa flopped back onto Haley's bed, careful to not jostle the outfit she'd painstakingly put together. "I can honestly say that the last year has been the most difficult of our marriage. I felt betrayed by Rob—and not just because of the rumors, but also because he didn't trust me enough to tell me what was going on in his head." She sighed. "But I also took on and then internalized *so* much. I was resentful, lonely, sad, and it wasn't all from our marriage, my childhood played a big role as well. Of course, I didn't think I needed to tell him that I was struggling. I thought he should just *know*." She huffed out a laugh. "Which is why we clearly needed therapy."

"But it helped," Haley said, lying down next to her.

"*Ohh* yeah. If only to just get us back on track. My tendencies are to pull inward and distance everyone around me—" She broke off. "Look at me going on and on. We're fine. Yes, we're a work in progress, but I can honestly say I'm happier now with Rob than I ever have been."

Haley leaned her head on Melissa's shoulder. "I'm so happy for you guys." She hesitated then decided that since Melissa had shared so much, she could bare her heart a little bit, too. "Also, I hear you. About the distancing stuff, I mean. Sometimes it's safer to be in my own head and heart and to not let anyone else in."

Miss rolled over and leaned up on one elbow. "But Sam is different."

"*So* different. God, I was so painfully awkward with him when I was younger, but now it's like so . . . so *easy* almost. He gets me, and for the first time ever, I'm seriously ready to jump and he wants to take it slow." Haley groaned. "And I know that's the responsible adult thing to do, but . . ."

"You don't care."

"I don't care." Haley *thunked* her head back. "Also, I'm horny."

Melissa tugged at a strand of Haley's hair. "Having dated a

particularly stubborn and protective man myself, I can say that you've got the right plan in mind. Corner him, blow his socks off with those sexy legs. Oh, and skip the underwear, bend over, and flash a little—"

"Miss!"

Melissa cackled. "But I'm only half-kidding. The man wants you, half the town witnessed just how much in that kiss last week. He just needs a push."

"In the form of no underwear under my dress."

A shrug. "What can I say? It works." She grinned. "Just promise me you won't heat up the dinner I brought for you guys until *after* he's seen the peep show."

Haley smacked her shoulder. "You're terrible."

"Maybe," Miss teased. "But I'm also getting lots of orgasms, so I think you want a piece of this pie." At her words, they both froze. Melissa grimaced. "Okay, so not the best word choice. I'm going to stop talking." She pushed off the bed, extended a hand to help Haley up, then pretended to knight her with one of the heels she'd pulled from the closet. "Go forth and jump Sam's bones."

TWENTY-TWO

Sam

Sam didn't think he'd ever slept that late . . . or definitely not since his teenage years. He'd shuffled through his front door the previous evening at a quarter past nine, dropped his jacket by the front door, stepped out of his boots, then stumbled into bed and hadn't moved until almost noon.

The benefit of approximately fourteen hours of sleep was that he had more energy than usual.

And he wanted to use that energy in a very specific way.

But he'd promised himself and Haley that they would take it slow, and in his mind that meant he was going to wait until her cast was off before they explored the physical stuff.

Physical stuff?

Fuck, he needed to get it together.

He wanted Haley. Badly. But she'd been through a lot with Brian, and that meant he needed to tread carefully. She needed to understand that—

He had fucking blue balls?

Yeah. That was a certainty.

But not the whole story because Haley had to know that she was beautiful and worthwhile and he wanted her so much that he'd been tempted to stroke himself to orgasm in the shower that afternoon.

Okay, no. She didn't need to know *that* part.

Just that—

Why was he waiting the full six weeks again?

"Respect, douche canoe," he muttered to himself in the mirror as he fixed his hair and slapped on some deodorant. "Haley deserves some fucking respect, not a meaningless one-night stand."

Except, it wouldn't be for one night, would it?

Because Haley was—

Fuck. He had the feeling that Haley was *everything*.

Hence, him not wanting to screw it all up. Sighing, Sam left the bathroom and headed to the kitchen for the flowers and the banana cream pie he'd begged Melissa to make.

He set the pie and flowers on the passenger's seat then rounded his SUV and forced his way into the driver's seat. His insurance had finally gotten back to him, and though he'd take a hit on the length of the loan, his new SUV would be delivered on Wednesday.

At least he wouldn't be in a wrestling match with his door multiple times a day.

Okay. Focus.

He'd pick Haley up and take her out to the diner or maybe for pizza, because it would have to be away from Haley's house and the temptation of stripping her naked and continuing where they'd left off in her kitchen the other day. But maybe afterward, he could trust himself enough to go inside for a drink and a slice of pie and not get her naked.

Not likely.

So, maybe the plan needed to be to get *her* naked but to keep himself clothed.

Yeah, *that* he thought he could do.

"Go team," he muttered, knowing he was way overthinking this, but not able to stop.

Not when Haley meant so much.

He kept his eyes peeled for deer as he navigated the short distance from his house to hers. Rob had been true to his word and the brush had been cut back, so Sam hadn't seen any kamikaze Bambis lately, but he wasn't exactly at the trust stage yet.

A few minutes later, he'd parked in Haley's driveway and was bounding up the stairs as she opened the door. He saw a glimpse of one bare knee resting on the scooter and . . .

He couldn't process the rest.

Because Haley was wearing a tight, short dress that highlighted every single curve.

"Hi," she said, her eyes warm, her smile satisfied, her breasts all but spilling out of the low V. "Is that Melissa's banana cream pie?"

A completely nonsexual question, but she bent over as she strained to see the container in his hand. Her breasts, fuck, but her breasts. She flicked her gaze back up to his. "Oh, Sam," she moaned. "I can't wait—"

And that was it for him.

He barely had the presence of mind to set the flowers and pie on the little bench that sat just inside her front door before he was reaching for her and sweeping her up into his arms.

Sam kicked the scooter aside then slammed—and locked this time—the door.

A heartbeat later his mouth was on hers.

He turned, pinning her back against the wood panel as he kissed her with every bit of pent-up lust from the last weeks.

Her breasts were soft against his chest, her thighs around his hips the best feeling in the fucking world. He slipped his tongue into her mouth, stroking it along hers until she finally pushed at his shoulders.

"Air," she gasped.

He kissed her again, long and deep and slow before nipping at the corner of her lips and then trailing his mouth down her neck and between her breasts.

Her fingernails bit into his shoulders as he nibbled and licked all of the exposed skin. "Sam," she groaned, encouraging him down while arching her breasts up. Her cast hit him in the back of the knee, and he sucked in a breath, shoring up his patience.

Fuck six weeks.

Tonight, he was going to make Haley come until she couldn't see straight.

"Please," she said, thighs clenching around his waist. "Please, don't stop."

"Shit," he gritted out, knowing that he wouldn't be able to reach everywhere he wanted to, knowing that she needed slow and steady and—she undulated against him, making stars flash behind his eyes, nearly destroying the hairsbreadth of patience he'd managed to steal—Haley needed a bed so her leg—

"Sam." Her mouth found his, and this time she took the lead, driving his desire to a fever pitch. His blood roiled beneath his skin, his cock was hard and aching and—

Forget the bed.

Couch. That worked.

He strode over, setting her down so her leg with the cast was stretched out along the cushions and the other was on the floor. The sight of her legs slightly spread, of her uninjured foot in a strappy black sandal—

"Fuck, you're beautiful," he said, his voice sounding like

he'd swallowed sandpaper, and he dove between her thighs, hitching her dress up and finding . . . *holy, fucking shit.* "Why aren't you wearing any underwear?"

Her teeth found her bottom lip, but there was heat in her gaze. "Because I knew I didn't need it."

His mind hazed over.

He couldn't think up a pithy one-liner, couldn't summon sweet words. Instead, he could only focus on how desperately he needed her to come on his tongue. So, he spread her thighs farther, bent, and pressed his mouth to her pussy. His cock twitched at the first taste of her, sweeter than the banana pie he'd brought, but then her hands were in his hair, tugging him closer, and Sam focused solely on Haley, on what made her groan and rub more firmly against him, on what made her breath catch, on what had her crying out.

He flicked his tongue against her clit and was rewarded by a moan. A finger inside and curling upward had her hips undulating, but she really liked it when he spread her wide and just licked her.

"Sam—mmm." Her head fell back to the cushions, her hips jerked forward. "*Fuck.* Mmm. I—"

He slipped his fingers under her ass and yanked her closer, flicking his tongue, licking her faster and faster until her hands tightened almost painfully in his hair.

And then he nipped.

Haley screamed as she came.

Fuck, but was that the best noise ever.

Her dress was shoved up around her hips, her pussy bare and glistening, her eyes were closed, a blush dusting the tops of her cheeks. She was the most beautiful woman he'd ever seen.

Ever. Hands down.

His heart pulsed.

Because he loved her.

Of course, he loved her.

What wasn't there to love?

For all the attraction, for all the lust raging inside him, Sam wanted Haley because she was as beautiful inside as she was on the outside.

Her eyes flicked open.

"Hi, sweetheart," he murmured.

"Hi, yourself," she said lazily, dropping her hands, which had still been in his hair, to his shoulders. "Come here."

He leaned up and kissed her.

"Nice surprise?" she asked when they broke apart.

"Nice surprise," he agreed and slid his hand up her bare thigh. "Very nice surprise."

"Good. *Sam*—" She sat up when his fingers teased the wet heat of her, nearly knocking her head against his.

"Shh," he said, shifting so he could gather her into his arms. "Now that I know what you like"—he stood—"I need to perfect my technique."

Haley groaned. "Good God that was terrible."

Sam suckled her bottom lip. "So, that's a no?"

"Fuck no, it's not a no," she said. "Your mouth on my pussy was perfect. It's your pickup lines that need work."

This woman. He had a boner that was aching and desperate, his every muscle tense, his mind hazed with desire, and still she made him laugh.

"I love you," he blurted.

Her face—*fuck,* but her face fell.

So, he kissed her.

Before she could really hear the words and panic, so she didn't pull back before he could prove himself. She met his tongue stroke for stroke, held him tightly as he walked them down the hall to her bedroom. But she tore her lips from his when he set her on the mattress. "Sam—"

He kissed her again.

Because he was the one panicking now. All his plans had been ruined with one blurted sentence. She would—

Haley turned her face from his, placed her hand over his mouth when he would have pressed it to hers again. "I—" He slid his hand back up her thigh, slipped fingers between. *In.*

"Sam—"

He knocked her hand aside and kissed her with every single one of the feelings that were roiling within him. If only he could convince her that—

"No!"

Sam froze, saw her face and jumped off her.

"Shit. Haley." He turned away, thrusting a hand through his hair. "Fuck. I'm sorry. I'll—"

"Will you shut the fuck up and listen to me?" she snapped, and cold tore through his every cell. He'd been here before. He put himself out there, and women didn't feel the same, and now he'd fucked up with Haley, and—

"Sam. Look at me."

He always took it like a man.

This time wouldn't be any different.

No matter that Haley made him feel more than all the other women combined.

He straightened his shoulders, spun around. He wouldn't make a scene. He'd go and leave her to her life and—

"I love you, too."

Her words were a gut punch, but the best kind.

"Oh."

Not the most eloquent response, but fuck, Haley loved him, too? How? Fuck. It was—

"Hey." She snapped her fingers. "Did I kill you?"

He shook his head, opened his mouth.

"Good," she interrupted. "Now, get back down here and don't renege on your promise of more oral sex."

Sam started to reply, started to ask if she was all right, to double check she was with him, but then Haley spread her legs and slid her fingers down between her thighs.

Fuck it all.

Talking could wait.

TWENTY-THREE

Haley

SAM DEFINITELY DIDN'T RENEGE on the oral sex front. He parked himself between her thighs and licked her until she absolutely lost her mind.

And then exploded into orgasm.

Twice.

But when he went to press his mouth to her after her third orgasm, she halted him with her hands on his shoulders. "Not on your life, mister."

"Mmm." He licked his lips. "I think I can convince you otherwise."

Haley shuddered. "My clit can't take it."

A brush of his fingers made her groan. "I think it can."

She let him stroke her once, okay three, okay maybe ten times more. But just as she was really starting to lose her mind, she reached into her nightstand and pulled out a condom.

"No, it can't. Here." She tore the packet open with her teeth and shoved it at him. "Inside me. Now."

Hesitation was rampant in his expression. "Maybe we should wait—"

Yeah, that wasn't happening.

She snaked her hand down and flicked open the button on his jeans. "Hal—*oh, fuck*—"

Oh, fuck was right because he was hot and hard and velvety.

"Yes." She slid herself down, executing a move that was quite acrobatic considering her bum foot, thank her very much.

"What—" His protest cut off as Haley sucked him into her mouth. "*Fuck.*" He groaned. "Baby, I—"

She gripped him with both hands and stroked.

Sam dropped his forehead to the bed above her shoulder, hips thrusting. But he only let her caress him for all of two heartbeats before he was tugging her hand away, tossing her back up onto the pillows. The condom was on a second later, and . . . he paused.

"You sure—"

Nope. No more talking. No way. No how.

Haley wrapped her good leg around his hip, lifted herself up, and—*oh . . . God . . . yes*—slid him inside of her.

He shuddered, locked his eyes onto hers. "Haley."

Just her name, but somehow a thousand emotions sewn into those five letters.

And she felt every single one of them, too, in her soul, her mind, her heart.

"I know," she murmured, reaching up to cup his face. "I know."

Because this was so much more than just an act. This meant something.

It meant *everything*.

"Kiss me," she said. "Show me."

And he did.

Sam pressed his lips to hers and began to move.

"About time you got your ass back in here!" Roxy said, rounding the high counter of the nurse's station to hug Haley on Friday the following week. "I've missed you. How's the leg?"

Haley gestured to her cast-covered ankle. "Still broken, but I've only got a few more weeks to go."

Roxy leaned against her desk, smoothed the long black tail of her hair over one shoulder. "Well, I hear that convalescence agrees with you."

Haley picked up a file, pretended to be firmly engrossed in the patient report she'd already read once. "I have absolutely no idea what you're talking about."

"Lies." Roxy plunked into the empty chair. "But I'm not going to pressure you, not when I can just get the gossip from Esther."

"Oh lord." Haley dropped the file.

The little old lady was trouble of epic proportions, and Haley and Sam's budding relationship was her preferred brand of trouble at the moment. She'd livestreamed their return to the diner—her words, not Haley's—then had featured their subsequent movie date, evening shopping trip, dinner at Melissa and Rob's, and even their visit to Roosevelt Ranch so Sam could perform an ultrasound on Kelly's horse on the town's Facebook group.

Stella was ten weeks along, fitting in with the timeline of Justin's horse menses faux pas.

Which was a statement Haley would have never thought she'd hear, let alone think.

Still, Kelly was thrilled, albeit very much a nervous horse mom. That in and of itself was hilarious, considering her job was running the breeding program. But Haley understood that some things couldn't be kept at a distance. She had a hard time seeing patients as simply patients sometimes—case in point, Melissa, who'd been her patient before she'd become her friend.

Because of that, Haley wasn't going to tease Kelly . . . not too much anyway.

Besides, she'd really enjoyed seeing Sam in action, loved how confident and capable he was when handling both Kelly *and* Stella, soothing both anxious females, human and horse, with equal aplomb. So, she was going to keep her mouth closed and try not to get banned from future veterinary house calls.

She'd also wondered why he didn't have pets of his own, considering how good he was with them. He'd always had a menagerie of cats, dogs, miniature pigs, and even geckos during high school and college.

Sam had shrugged when she asked. "I had to put my last dog down a few years ago, and I just decided that I'd wait until I had more spare time before I got another one. Plus, and this will sound bad, but after taking care of everyone else's animals all day, sometimes I just want to go home and not worry about anything but myself."

"That makes total sense," she'd told him. "Sometimes I just want to leave someone choking when I see them in a restaurant because I want to not worry about anything."

He'd almost swerved the truck off the road, so quickly his gaze had snapped to hers.

"I joke," she'd said, palms facing out.

Sam had scowled. "Not funny." A pause before his lips twitched. "Is this part of that dark ER humor?"

"Probably." She'd winced. "No, definitely."

"Noted," he said, but had rubbed the dashboard of his new SUV lovingly. "You are also now banned from joking while driving."

A nod. "No JWD. Got it."

And in one of those perfect moments, he'd laced his fingers

through hers and glanced down at her, hazel eyes a warm mix of brown and gold and green. "I love you."

Her breath had caught, her heart fluttered, and she'd said, "I love you, too."

Simple moments and yet they meant so much. He was just—

"Earth to Haley Bear!" Roxy called, bumping Haley's chair with her own. "Shake off the Sam fog and get to work."

Since she was technically off the clock and waiting for Sam to come pick her up, Haley wasn't exactly worried about her productivity. What concerned her more was the fact that the nickname *Haley Bear* had apparently caught on.

Next time she saw Esther, she was going to take her phone away.

That woman had absolutely no shame.

"Foxy Roxy," Haley said.

Roxy might be younger than her, but they'd both grown up in Darlington and were still close enough in age that Haley knew own Roxy's embarrassing nickname. Thus, one mention of *Foxy Roxy* was all it took to get the other woman to behave.

That and: "Just remember, my list of embarrassing details about you doesn't end with nicknames."

Roxy nodded rapidly. "No Haley Bear." Another nod. "Got it."

Haley lifted her fingers, pointing them at her own eyes then in Roxy's direction. "Make sure you don't forget it. Otherwise I might have to let Esther know who spray-painted Old-Man McDavid's cow in high school."

"You *wouldn't*."

Haley only raised a brow in response.

"You would. Damn. You're mean, Haley Donovan."

She nodded. "And don't you forget it."

"I won't." Roxy's department phone rang, calling an end to

her short break, and she pushed to her feet. They were surprisingly busy as they moved into the evening shift, but at least that would make the time go by fast. "Anyway," Roxy said. "This is my Friday, so I won't see you until next week." She waved and started hurrying down the hall, pausing only to call over her shoulder, "Make sure you share all your good Sam time with Esther. I need to live vicariously."

"Hilarious," Haley muttered, glancing down at her phone screen. Sam was supposed to have been there twenty minutes ago, and he hadn't responded to her text saying she had finished up and was ready to go whenever.

He'd probably had to deal with an emergency himself or a late patient. That normally wouldn't have been an issue with her, medicine—whether for people or animals—didn't always run on a perfect schedule. But he'd also insisted on dropping her off that morning since she couldn't drive yet, and now she was stuck.

Maybe Maggie or Melissa could come pick her up. She could catch up with Sam later.

She pulled out her phone, texted her sister first, and received a response barely thirty seconds later.

In Salt Lake for Ashley's dance tournament. I'm sorry.
I'd order Tim to come get you, but he's in New York for a
work trip.

Damn. After telling her sister not to worry about it, she tried Melissa next. Melissa's producer texted back a few minutes later.

Melissa will be done filming in two hours.

Shit. She'd forgotten her friend was back at Roosevelt

Ranch filming the latest season of her cooking show. Melissa was a hell of a cook, hence the reason she'd been so excited when Sam had brought over her signature banana cream pie the other day. After sending a quick apology for interrupting, Haley sat back in her chair and considered what to do.

"Hey." Haley glanced up at the sound of Julian's voice. He'd been relieved by the night shift doctor and had his lab coat over one arm and his keys in his other hand. "Your shift ended a half hour ago. Everything okay?"

"Fine. I'm just waiting for Sam." She held up her phone. "He's running behind."

"Oh, well I'm heading out. Did you want a ride?"

"Do you mind?"

Julian rolled his eyes. "I wouldn't have offered if I minded." He tilted his head toward the doors. "Come on, Mario Kart."

"That nickname better not stick," she grumbled and hopped onto her scooter to follow him out to his car.

"You're welcome," he deadpanned, but held open his car door for her as she slowly and ungracefully maneuvered herself into the passenger's seat. A tug on the end of her ponytail had her glancing up and glaring when she saw him bite back a smile. "Not going to bring any suicidal deer down on me, are you?"

She buckled her seat belt. "You're lucky you're a good doctor."

He rounded the car, sat in his own seat, and strapped in. "Everyone's lucky I'm a great doctor."

"And modest, too."

Julian snorted. "Damn right."

"Just drive, Jeeves. You're not funny."

He backed out of the parking spot. "Except I am."

Haley sighed. She had the feeling this was going to be a long ride home.

TWENTY-FOUR

Sam

HIS GAZE WAS TRACKING the seconds on the clock in the back of the clinic. Two more appointments and then he and Haley could have the rest of the night together. Well, actually the whole weekend. He'd blocked his Friday and Saturday, Michelle having offered to give him a break, and the clinic was closed on Sunday.

After the business of the last week, Sam was definitely ready for some alone time with Haley.

He'd dropped her at work that morning and was anxious to know how things had gone. Was she going stir crazy on her first day back, not being able to do more than glorified filing and the odd consult? Or was she just satisfied being out of the house?

Well, he wouldn't be able to discover the answer to either of those questions until he got his shit done.

Shit, quite literally . . . in one of the cases anyway.

They'd had a golden retriever with an intestinal blockage the previous day. The pup had required surgery and follow up, and they were now waiting for him to move his bowels before he could go home.

Sam's job was so glamorous.

Snorting, he poked his head in on the vet tech who was walking Buddy. She shook her head.

Damn. So, another night in the hospital with monitoring for Buddy, and then Michelle could check on him in the morning.

His last appointment of the day was a simple one in some ways and extremely complicated in others. He only needed to give a few routine vaccines. The complication came in the form of a litter of six eight-week-old kittens.

He spent the last hour of his day, quite literally, herding cats.

By the time he escaped the room of kittens, he'd been scratched, bitten, and licked. Definitely the combination he *wanted*, unfortunately it wasn't with the species—or person—he wanted.

Sam spent a few minutes washing up and checking in with his overnight staff before he got into his SUV and headed for the hospital.

Halfway there, he remembered the present he'd left at his house for Haley. His eyes flicked to the clock, saw he still had a half hour until he had to pick her up from her shift.

Plenty of time.

Plus, she would be exhausted and starving after her first day back.

He had to think that banana cream pie would be a welcome addition. Okay, so he knew it would be, even if the slice he had wasn't Melissa's recipe. Rather it was something Henry was introducing at the diner. He'd given Sam a piece earlier that day after he'd gone to the diner for lunch.

"Should have brought it to work with me," he muttered as he drove down the narrow two-lane road. Then he would have been able to give Haley her treat without having to make this drive.

Oh well. He hadn't exactly been thinking straight, not after Haley had sent him a few very suggestive texts that had all but melted his brain.

Sam turned onto Old Creek Road, his mind full of those sensual promises.

She was going to stay at his house for the first time that night, and he had all sorts of plans for the various services in his house. The kitchen counter, the shower, the hot tub, the washing machine, the shoe rack—

Well, his mind might be a little overstimulated, but at least it had creativity.

With a snort, he took one hand from the wheel and pressed the knob to turn on the radio. Nothing happened.

"What?" His gaze scanned the screen for a second before focusing back on the road. Nothing had changed with the stereo, despite the new SUV, so it wasn't operator error.

He pressed the knob again.

And silence.

"Hmm." He twisted the dial up—nothing—and down— nothing. He turned the other dial, pressed other buttons.

Still, the cab of his vehicle was silent.

Whatever, he didn't need music anyway. He was almost to his house and would fiddle with the system there. If nothing worked, he'd get the dealer to fix it.

See? Look at him. The man with the plan.

Hopefully, Haley would appreciate all his plans. Though— he couldn't hold back his smirk—there had been no *hopefully* with regards to his scheming the previous night. She'd loved them, especially the part where he'd managed to get them both naked.

Naked time was seriously the best time.

If Haley had heard any bit of his last thoughts, Sam knew he'd never live it down, but she *wasn't* there and so that meant he had carte blanche to imagine all the ways he wanted to bring her to orgasm.

And there were many.

With his mouth—her standing with one leg over his shoulder, him kneeling between her thighs. With his fingers—her in that dress again, no panties of course, him sliding his hand up her bare thigh and teasing her to a slow and intense orgasm. With his cock—

"Fuck!"

Two things happened at once.

One, the kamikaze deer had returned, and two, his radio blared to life, static blasting through the speakers and making him jerk the wheel.

He'd been so busy imaging all the ways he'd like to have Haley in his bed that he'd missed Suicidal Bambi on the side of the road. That combined with the jar of sound meant that—

He was fucked.

Sam tried to jerk the wheel back to center, but it was too late. His brand-new SUV was heading straight for the ditch on the side of Old Creek Road.

He slammed on the brakes.

The deer jumped clear of his bumper at the same moment his tires shuddered and tried to find purchase on the shoulder.

Purchase wasn't to be found.

The front wheels plowed into the ditch, slamming him forward against the steering wheel.

Everything went black.

TWENTY-FIVE

Haley

SHE GLANCED down at her phone screen in worry. She'd texted Sam for the second time and had yet to receive a response.

That in and of itself was unusual.

What was also unusual? The churning in her gut.

Perhaps in the past she might have thought that Sam was ignoring her, punishing her for some perceived slight like Brian used to. But Sam wasn't like that, and . . . she was worried.

"Why don't you call the vet clinic if you think something is wrong?" Julian asked as they got off the highway and drove through downtown Darlington. "That way, if he did get caught up with a patient, you'll know and can relax."

Haley gaped over at him. "How'd you get so smart?" she blurted before realizing the sentiment would make him even more arrogant.

He grinned. "I was born this way."

Rolling her eyes, she dialed the number to Sam's office. His receptionist Jane picked up. "Darlington Veterinary, how can I help you?"

"Hi, Jane," she said. "It's Haley. Is Sam still there?"

There was a pause. "Umm no, Haley. Sam left to get you"—there was a pause as though Jane were leaning over to check the clock—"over an hour ago."

The worry, the churning in her stomach, intensified.

Because something was wrong.

Very, very wrong.

She barely processed thanking Jane, just hung up and dialed Sam's number. It rang once and went straight to voice mail.

"Nothing?" Julian asked.

Haley shook her head. "Nothing." A beat as she dialed again. Got voice mail again. "He's probably fine. Just—"

"Let's keep going to your house," Julian said. "We can start our search from there."

"*Our* search?" Her gaze found his.

Julian nodded. "I'm not going to leave my best nurse to handle things on her own."

"Your best nurse?" She attempted to play along, even as she dialed Sam's number for a third time, got his voice mail for a third time.

Fuck.

Something was seriously wrong. She knew it.

Julian touched her shoulder. "He's fine. I'm sure this is just a misunderstanding.

But he didn't sound sure. Not at all.

Julian paused at the stop sign then turned right onto Old Creek Road. "Sometimes cell coverage is bad out here—"

His words cut off as they came around a corner and saw an SUV—*Sam's* SUV, plowed into the ditch on the side of the road.

Smoke rose from beneath the hood, glass glittered across the roadway, and . . . there was no sign of Sam.

Julian skidded the car to a stop, threw on the hazards. "Stay here."

Then he was out of the car and sprinting for the SUV.

Haley opened her door and hopped out, reaching into the back seat to grab the med kit she knew Julian stored there. Throwing it over her shoulder, she kept as much of her weight as possible off her ankle as she ran after Julian. Which wasn't a lot, given the shooting pain up her leg.

She ignored it.

Because the whole area smelled like gas.

Julian had opened the driver's door by the time she reached him and was feeling for Sam's pulse.

Please, God, let there be a pulse.

"Unconscious," he said, and she relaxed, dropping the kit and extracting a collar. They'd need to immobilize him before they moved him. Sam took the collar and secured it. "Back up. I need to move him in case the gas catches."

Haley hopped away, extracting her phone and dialing 9-1-1, as Julian lifted Sam from the SUV and carried him a safe distance away. Dispatch picked up her call, and she gave them the rundown of injuries as Julian called them out to her.

It was a good thing Julian moved Sam because the moment they heard sirens in the background, flames burst from beneath the SUV's hood.

Haley had knelt next to Sam, helping Julian by putting pressure on a cut on Sam's shoulder, so she saw the first moment Sam's eyes opened.

"Fucking deer," he groaned and started to sit up.

They kept him in place, but not before he saw the flaming ball of fire that was his new SUV. Sam's eyes flashed wide.

"That's not—" Heat radiated in the space around. "Oh, fuck me, it *is*."

Haley thought he was referring to the brand-new SUV going up in flames, but then she saw where his gaze was focused.

"Holy—"

Julian's jaw dropped open.

Because a family of deer stood directly in the middle of the road, staring at them, their beady eyes almost menacing.

"Deer," Julian muttered. "Fucking deer."

The sirens grew louder, and the deer held their ground for one long moment before jumping the barrier and hopping off into the nearby field.

A fire truck roared to a stop beside them, and after checking to make sure Sam was good, that Julian and Haley had it under control until the ambulance arrived, they immediately went to work on the fire.

"Deer trying to kill me," Sam muttered, eyes fluttering closed, limbs going limp.

"He's fine," Julian reassured her. "But I swear, he might actually be right. Those deer might seriously be trying to murder him."

TWENTY-SIX

Sam

IT WAS NEARLY a week later before Sam was able to sort out in his mind exactly what had happened. One minute he'd been heading to pick up Haley's pie, and the next he was waking up in the hospital with a concussion.

He didn't remember the roadside rescue or the apparent attempted killing by the murderous deer.

He remembered pie, a soft hand in his, and kind blue eyes staring down at him while he lay in a hospital bed.

Lucky for him, his bodily injuries were minimal. Concussion aside, he didn't have any broken bones or cuts requiring sutures. He just had his slightly addled brain and nightmares about deer lying in wait on the side of the room.

Thankfully, his buddy Dan at Fish and Game had come down to investigate the issue. It turned out that a fawn was trapped behind the fence of the ranch next to his house. The deer were hanging around close to the road because the mother deer wouldn't leave her baby.

"That's so sweet," Haley said, sitting next to him on the couch as Dan explained the problem and how they were going to make it safer for them to drive.

"Tell that to my SUV," he muttered. Or his head.

"Shh," Haley said. "Don't ruin it."

Dan shook their hands then stood, and Haley tried to follow suit. Sam pressed her back into the couch with narrowed eyes. "Don't you dare. That ankle needs rest."

She'd set herself back a week of recovery after her hop-a-long road escapades, but luckily none of the bones in her leg had been reinjured significantly.

"Samwise," she began.

"Haley Bear," he warned, cutting her off. "Don't start with me."

She crossed her arms, but her lips had curved. "You're sexy when you're bossy." Dan snorted, and she waggled her fingers at him. "Bye now! Thanks for saving us from the homicidal deer."

"A good woman," Dan said as Sam walked him out.

"Yes." He paused, opened the front door. "She's also mine."

"The concussion turned him into a caveman, Dan," Haley called. "Don't mind him!"

Dan chuckled and hesitated on the threshold. "Still yours?" he asked. "Despite the smart mouth?"

Sam couldn't hold back his smile. "Still mine. Always and forever."

Haley chimed in. "Also, he loves my smart mouth."

Dan grinned and said, "He ever screws up, sweetheart, and I'm next in line. I like my women with smart mouths and a little fire under the surface."

"Go away," Sam said and slammed the door.

Haley gasped, probably because that had been rude as fuck, but Sam found he didn't give a damn, not when after days of doctors and visitors and gossipmongers—hello, Esther—he finally had his woman alone.

"Hi," she said when he crossed back over to her. "Gonna kick me out now, too?"

He rolled his eyes, gathered her into his arms. "Didn't you hear what I said?"

"You mean the 'mine and always and forever' stuff?" She shrugged. "I thought that was just a ploy to get Dan to leave."

For a moment, she seemed so uncertain and sad that Sam almost rushed to reassure her. But then he saw the twinkle in her blue eyes, the twitching of her lips.

"Not funny."

"Too much?" she asked.

"Never," he told her. "You'll never be too much for me." He paused. "But also, yes, I want you for forever, and no, it's not a joke or a ploy. I love you, sweetheart and . . ."

She yawned, snuggled close. "And insert romantic words here?"

"Yes, *exactly* that," he teased and kissed the top of her head. "Pretend I just recited *all* the best romantic lines and that you fell madly in love with me."

"Too late," she said with another yawn. "I was already madly in love with you. Also—"

She curled into his side when he lay down on the couch, and when she didn't add anything further he asked, "You also what?"

"I want the always and forever."

He grinned.

"With Henry," she added with a smirk. "Because his banana cream pie might be even better than Melissa's."

Sam growled, and she burst into chuckles, and he couldn't resist following suit, not when he loved the sound of her laughter and her smile and even her terrible—truly *terrible*—attempts at humor.

He brushed a lock of her hair off her forehead and said, "You'll always keep me on my toes, won't you?"

Her laughter cut off, serious blue eyes meeting his. "Why do you say that like it's a good thing?"

"Because it is, sweetheart."

"Even though I'm a pain in the ass?"

He kissed her. "But you're *my* pain in the ass."

Haley grinned. "Such romance."

"You're my *beautiful* pain in the ass?"

"Better," she said, laughter in her words.

"I'll keep working on it," he quipped.

She cupped his cheeks. "I love you, Sam Johnson. Don't ever change."

And he knew the one thing that would never change was how much he loved this woman.

"Now"—she tried to affect a stern expression and failed miserably—"go get me that banana pie from the fridge."

He kissed that laughing mouth . . . and got up to get the pie.

EPILOGUE

HENRY

HENRY WIPED down the final table, beyond ready to go home and crash after a busy Sunday evening cooking at the diner.

He'd already flicked off the "Open" sign and dimmed the lights. The kitchen had been scrubbed and reset for the next morning's breakfast rush. He'd sent Tilly off about an hour before—she'd had a date and he didn't mind sweeping up or stocking the tables with all of the necessities for the next day.

Paper napkins, ketchup, salt and pepper, sugar. They weren't what had been on the tables in the Michelin-starred restaurant he'd cooked at while living in New York City several years before, but they were his childhood.

His way of feeling close to his dad.

God, he missed his dad.

The bell hanging on the front door rang, and he mentally cursed at having forgotten to lock it.

Talk about a beginner mistake.

He'd worked half his childhood in the diner, had closed it down more times than he could count.

And somehow, he'd forgotten to lock the front door.

"I'm sorry, we're closed," he said and reached to straighten a saltshaker that was askew.

"So, this is your place, is it?" The softly accented voice made him freeze.

Italian. Warm Tuscan sunlight, softly rolling hills through wine country. Cheese and pasta and pizza and . . . *her*.

He accidentally knocked the shaker to the floor. It didn't break because this was a family place and they'd learned long ago that plastic was safer with the kiddos, but Henry watched in slow horror as the lid popped off and salt spread out on the tile.

Though his horror didn't come from the spilled salt.

No. It came from the fact that she was there.

He turned. Saw he hadn't been mistaken.

She was there.

Isabella Mariano was in Darlington, Utah. Inside his diner.

"*Buona notte*, Henry."

He'd last seen her as she'd gotten on a plane heading the opposite direction from where he'd needed her, flying away when he'd asked her to come with him, bolting when his heart had been shattering.

"Isabella," he said coldly.

If she noticed his tone, then she didn't comment on it.

Then again, she was good at that.

"What are you doing here?" he prompted when she didn't say anything further.

She swept through, more beautiful than ever, brown hair falling in perfect waves, killer body in sleek designer clothes, huge diamond on her left ring finger sparkling in the dim light.

Diamond ring.

On her left hand.

He processed that, but her words still hit him like a two-by-four to the temple.

"I want you to cater my wedding."

—Regret at Roosevelt Ranch Now Available

ROOSEVELT RANCH SERIES

Disaster at Roosevelt Ranch

Heartbreak at Roosevelt Ranch

Collision at Roosevelt Ranch

Regret at Roosevelt Ranch

Desire at Roosevelt Ranch

Did you miss any of the other Roosevelt Ranch books? Check out excerpts from the series below or find the full series here: amazon.com/gp/product/B07Q8VRK9Y

DISASTER AT ROOSEVELT RANCH
Book One
(books2read.com/DARR)

I had never thought of a plus sign as a bad thing.

Of course, I'd never had one show up on a stick I'd peed on. Kudos to me, that changed today.

My knees wobbled, and the idiotic white piece of plastic rattled as I set it on the scarred Formica countertop.

Brown eyes—mine—stared back at me accusingly in the mirror. "You've done it now."

A baby.

My hand found my stomach. Still flat, still the same.

Even though so much had changed.

The bathroom door rattled as a fist slammed against the thin plank of wood. "Move it, Kel! Food's up and your tables are restless."

"Coming!" I called as I wrapped the test in a paper towel before shoving it deep into my purse.

I couldn't leave it here. Not where anyone—where *Henry*— might see it. He would get his back up, storm out to the ranch where he-who-must-not-be-named lived, and drag the no-good, low down piece of crap into town for a proper whooping.

And I might just want to let him.

With a sigh, I washed my hands and left the bathroom.

It was my own fault. I knew the type of man Rex was.

I'd fallen into his bed anyway.

"Regret never fails to burn like a mother," I muttered as I swept into the kitchen, grabbed the plates from the pass, and started hustling toward my table.

"What was that?" Henry asked as he flipped a burger.

"Nothing." I hefted the tray filled with six plates and various food accessories—ketchup, extra dressing, and napkins—with practiced ease.

Oh, God. I was going to be huge and pregnant and . . . waiting tables.

Good luck to the customers, because I lacked the sincerity and cheerfulness that seemed to come naturally to most waitresses on a normal day. I could only imagine what was going to happen when my hormones raged.

Using my back, I pushed through the swinging door and promptly stumbled to a stop.

He was here. *Rex* was here.

Stupidly, my heart raced. He'd changed his mind. He'd—

The man's eyes flicked to mine, completely unrecognizing and indifferent. My momentary burst of hope disintegrated.

He was going to pretend not to know me? To not *recognize* me?

The jerk! The rotten—

Except . . . there was something off about him. I squinted, trying to discern the change, but the tray was taking its toll on my arms. I tore my gaze away from Rex to practically hurl the dishes at my customers.

"Anything else?" I asked, and was thankful when there weren't any requests.

Two seconds later, I was in front of Rex.

Who wasn't *actually* Rex.

Oh, he was the right height and had the same square jaw

and the same gorgeous, sun-kissed skin, but *this* man wasn't the one I'd slept with.

"Hi," he said, his green eyes warm. They were a brilliant emerald and just as inviting as they'd been in the picture I'd seen on Rex's desk. "Can I just sit anywhere?"

My nod was jerky. "I'll get you a menu."

Fingers brushed my arm—calloused fingers that felt both familiar and different.

"You okay?"

I forced a smile, my stomach churning. This could *not* be happening. "Just perfect—"

And that was the moment I puked all over Rex's twin's shoes.

—Get your copy books2read.com/DARR.

HEARTBREAK AT ROOSEVELT RANCH
Book Two
(books2read.com/HARR)

I straightened from putting the last plate into the dishwasher and stretched for a towel to wipe my hands. I was exhausted after twenty-four straight hours with the kids, and Rob still wasn't home. Not to mention, I needed to make cupcakes for Max's school—and somehow do it without sugar.

So the ensuing crash upstairs was not welcome.

Dropping the towel, I whisper-sprinted up to the second floor—running on tiptoes while hopping, leaping, and skipping over every toy obstacle, creaky floorboard, and rogue crayon along the way.

The light was on in Max's room, and considering that I had

made this trek a half dozen times in the last hour, I was out of patience.

"You need to go to sleep," I growled, throwing open the door, my fierce mom glare already in place.

Except the devil child *was* asleep.

He'd fallen out of bed, crashed onto an entire village of Legos—scattering them to hell and back—and was dead asleep.

My heart gave a little squeeze even as the logical part of me recognized the giant mess I'd be picking up tomorrow.

It was just that face.

A cupid's bow of bright pink lips, slightly parted, rosy cheeks, and mussed hair. The boy was cute, and it was hard to believe he was part of me, that he'd come from my body.

I clucked my tongue at myself, knowing I was being ridiculous and romantic and *Melissa-like* because I'd spent the day with Kelly and her toddler, Abby.

My baby sister had a baby. And a man. And was all grown up—

Oh God. There I went with the tears again.

Swiping a finger under each eye, I navigated the minefield of toys as I made my way over to Max. I gave an internal grunt as I lifted the little—or not so little, anymore—monkey and tucked him back into bed.

One hastily constructed barrier of pillows and blankets and stuffed Minecraft toys later, and I was heading back out of the room.

I flicked the light off, started to leave—

"Too dark, Mommy," he murmured.

A sigh. Back on it went. "Good night, sweetheart."

"Night."

This time I made it to the top of the stairs before a sound stopped me.

It wasn't the kids. No. This was more like . . . buzzing?

I cocked my head and listened, then made my way to my bedroom, a growing pile of toys in my arms as I went.

The door was open, and I walked inside, dumping the pile on the coverlet before stopping to pinpoint the sound.

I felt my pockets for my cell. Not even two days before, I'd scoured the house for my phone, it somehow having fallen out of my pocket, ending up under the dresser. It had taken darn near fifty calls and a search of the entire house before I'd found it.

Those locating apps were all well and good, but they couldn't tell a person which room in a house their phone was. Which meant the app, for my day-to-day exploits, was pretty much useless.

I hardly left home at all except for the kids' activities and school pickup or drop off.

Or if Rob needed something down at the station.

And that was fine. My place was at home. The kids needed me, Rob needed me. It was just that sometimes . . .

No. Don't get sidetracked.

My phone *was* in my pocket. The sound wasn't coming from beneath the dresser.

It was coming from the bed.

I peered under, saw nothing, and I was reaching for Rob's flashlight in his nightstand when I realized where exactly the noise was originating from.

My hand slid between the mattress and box spring, jumping a little when the object buzzed against my fingers.

"What—?" I pulled it out, saw it was an older-looking iPhone. Why was there—

Then I saw the texts. An entire screen worth of them.

And my heart froze solid.

I'm heading to the hotel.

Where are you?

Don't keep me waiting, honey.

I need you.

The question wasn't why Rob had hidden a phone under his side of the mattress. It was why someone named Celeste was calling him honey and telling *my* husband that she needed him.

Downstairs, I heard the garage door rumble open and close, the clink of Rob's keys on the kitchen counter. "Miss?" he called softly up the stairs.

My voice was gone, my throat tight. My eyes burned, and still, I held the phone. It wasn't until I heard him walking down the hall to the bedroom that I sprang into motion.

I shoved the phone back under the mattress and scooped up the toys.

Rob stopped short in the doorway. "Oh." He smiled. "I called you."

"Sorry, I was cleaning."

He touched my cheek, slid past me. "You don't have to do that."

"It's my job," I said brightly, and if it was too bright then what did it matter anyway?

My husband was moving toward the bathroom, already unbuttoning his shirt. "Is there a plate for me?"

I turned, saw he'd paused, and forced a smile. "Yup. I'll heat it up for you."

"Thanks, love."

"Of course." I walked out of the bedroom but didn't go downstairs.

Instead, I hesitated in the hall, silent and waiting.

And my gut tied itself into knots when I heard Rob's footfalls across the carpet, the slide of his hand beneath the mattress as he pulled out the phone.

—Get your copy at books2read.com/HARR.

REGRET AT ROOSEVELT RANCH
Book Four
(books2read.com/RARR)

Henry

Henry wiped down the final table. He was beyond ready to go home and crash after a busy Sunday evening cooking at the diner.

He'd already flicked off the neon "Open" sign and dimmed the lights. The kitchen had been scrubbed and reset for the next morning's breakfast rush, and he'd sent Tilly off about an hour earlier—she'd had a date, and Henry didn't mind sweeping up or stocking the tables with all the necessities for the next day.

Paper napkins, ketchup, salt and pepper, sugar. They weren't what had been on the tables in the Michelin-starred restaurant he'd cooked at while living in New York five years before, but they were his childhood.

His way of feeling close to his dad.

God, he missed his dad.

The bell hanging on the front door rang, and he mentally cursed at having forgotten to lock it.

Beginner mistake.

He'd worked half his childhood in the diner, had closed it down more times than he could count.

And somehow, he'd forgotten to lock the front door.

Hopeless.

"I'm sorry, we're closed," he said, deliberately not looking as he reached to straighten a salt shaker that was slightly askew.

"So, this is your place, is it?" The softly accented voice made him freeze.

Italy. Warm Tuscan sunlight, softly rolling hills through wine country. Cheese and pasta and pizza and . . . *her*.

He accidentally knocked the shaker to the floor. It didn't break because this was a family place and they'd learned long ago that plastic was safer with the kiddos, but Henry watched in slow horror as the lid popped off and salt spread out on the tile floor.

Though his horror didn't come from the spilled salt.

No. It came from the fact that she was there.

He turned. Saw for sure he hadn't been mistaken.

She was there.

Isabella Mariano was in Darlington, Utah. Inside his restaurant.

"*Buona notte*, Henry."

He'd last seen her as she'd gotten on a plane heading the opposite direction of where he'd needed her, flying away when he'd asked her to stay, bolting while his heart had been left to shatter.

"Isabella," he said coldly.

If she noticed his tone, she didn't comment on it.

Then again, she was good at that.

"What are you doing here?" he prompted when she didn't say anything further.

She swept over to him, heels clicking on the tile floor, more beautiful than ever. Her brown hair fell in perfect waves, her killer body was clad in sleek designer clothes, and a diamond ring on her left ring finger sparkled in the dim light.

Diamond ring.

On her left hand.

He processed that, but her words still hit him like a two-by-four to the temple.

"I want you to cater my wedding."

—Get your copy at books2read.com/RARR

DESIRE AT ROOSEVELT RANCH
Book Five
(books2read.com/DesireARR)

Rex

He drove down the dark road, trying to figure out why he was still in Darlington, Utah almost two months after he'd deposited Bella back with her one true love, Henry.

Barf.

Love was for idiots.

Or pussies.

Or people who were insanely, sickeningly happy.

Ugh.

Rex was jealous. He knew it. He embraced it.

But that didn't change the fact he wasn't the kind of person who fell in love. Or rather, he didn't *allow* himself to fall in love. He'd seen the way his father had loved his mother—a touching Hollywood scene if there ever was one, filled with so much devotion and affection that when she'd died, he'd changed.

Part of him had died, too.

And so Rex and Justin had lost *both* parents.

That was the troubling part of so-called happily ever afters.

They never lasted.

Rex sighed because the real casualties in those failed or aborted happy endings were the kids. *They* suffered. *They* lost it all. *They*—

"Fuck!" he said and swerved, almost clipping the car pulled barely on the shoulder.

No hazard lights flashing. No flares. Nothing but a dark shape silhouetted against the moonlight. Were they trying to get themselves killed?

He slowed and turned around, heading back to the parked car.

His tirade about responsibility was on the tip of his tongue and—*ha*—if anyone even knew that *he'd* thought the word responsibility, they would have keeled over and dropped dead.

Responsibility and Rex Roosevelt did not belong in the same sentence.

He was the screw-up.

He was the bad guy.

He was pulling over behind the car.

Rex parked behind them and turned on his hazard lights before getting out. He'd extended a hand to knock when he saw the woman inside. Spot-lit by his car's headlights, she looked like an angel with pale blonde hair and delicate features.

Or at least from the glimpse he caught, they *seemed* delicate.

He only caught hints of a pert nose, plump lips, and a petite chin because she was spending a lot of time banging her face against the steering wheel.

Rex hesitated and almost turned away, leaving her to whatever sort of mental breakdown she was determined to have, but just as he'd taken a step back toward his car, his conscience pinged.

The annoying bastard had been all too busy lately.

He sighed but knew he couldn't leave her, and so he blew out a breath, raised his hand, and knocked on the window.

The woman inside jumped.

Her gaze shot to his for one long moment before her eyes slid closed, head dropping down to the steering wheel.

But Rex barely noticed.

Because one look from *her,* and he'd felt like he'd been struck over the head by a two-by-four.

Or maybe hit in the ass by Cupid's arrow.

She was . . . different . . . wonderful . . .

And he wanted her.

—Desire at Roosevelt Ranch coming November 17th

ACKNOWLEDGMENTS

This is always the point in every book that I'm reminded of exactly how many people it takes to turn my books into something that you as readers can enjoy! I quite literally could not do it without you, KC. Thank you for looking at dozens of cover options and potential titles and snorting along with my inner teenage boy. I also want to send a big thank you out to Julie, Kay, and Christine who shape my books into something palpable. And Jena! Thank you for the fabulous covers. *Always*. Also, thank you Tiffany for snapping the pic of the Hubs and me that's on the front cover of this book. When I saw it, I knew it was perfect for this series, so thanks for letting me use it! Last, to the Hubs and my little (or not so little anymore) munchkins, I love you guys. Thanks for helping me along with this crazy endeavor.

And thank YOU for reading Collision at Roosevelt Ranch! I loved being able to jump back into Darlington and all things Roosevelt Ranch and horses and Melissa and Kelly! If you'd like to catch up on all my other releases, please check out my website: www.elisefaber.com. There you can sign up for my newsletter (with monthly bookish giveaways, woohoo!), check out my other books (everything from hockey romance to contemporary stand alones), and get to know more about my dorky self (hockey, chocolate, Star Wars . . . okay, I'm pretty boring).

You can also find me on Facebook (@elisefaberauthor), via my FB fan group (www.facebook.com/group/fabinators), or Instagram (@elisefaber). I look forward to talking with you soon!
Love you guys!
—XOXO,
E

ALSO BY ELISE FABER

(see a full listing and descriptions at www.elisefaber.com)

Roosevelt Ranch Series (all stand alone)

Disaster at Roosevelt Ranch

Heartbreak at Roosevelt Ranch

Collision at Roosevelt Ranch

Regret at Roosevelt Ranch

Desire at Roosevelt Ranch (Nov 17, 2019)

Billionaire's Club (all stand alone)

Bad Night Stand

Bad Breakup

Bad Husband

Bad Hookup

Bad Divorce

Bad Fiancé

Bad Boyfriend (Jan 2020)

Gold Hockey (all stand alone)

Blocked

Backhand

Boarding

Benched

Breakaway

Breakout (Dec 2019)

Life Sucks Series (all stand alone)

Train Wreck

Phoenix Series (read in order)

Phoenix Rising

Dark Phoenix

Phoenix Freed

Phoenix: LexTal Chronicles (rereleasing soon, stand alone, Phoenix world)

From Ashes

KTS Series

Fire and Ice (Hurt Anthology, stand alone)

ABOUT THE AUTHOR

USA Today bestselling author, Elise Faber, loves chocolate, Star Wars, Harry Potter, and hockey (the order depending on the day and how well her team -- the Sharks! -- are playing). She and her husband also play as much hockey as they can squeeze into their schedules, so much so that their typical date night is spent on the ice. Elise is the mom to two exuberant boys and lives in Northern California. Connect with her in her Facebook group, the Fabinators or find more information about her books at www.elisefaber.com.

- facebook.com/elisefaberauthor
- amazon.com/author/elisefaber
- bookbub.com/profile/elise-faber
- instagram.com/elisefaber
- goodreads.com/elisefaber
- pinterest.com/elisefaberwrite